ALLEY OF THE DOLLS

Also by the author

MisStep

Seeders

Pemako Burning

The Nyrian Transmission

Pirates Come Down

American Dreamer

Tomorrow's History

Gods and Dreamers

Journey to the Stars (stories)

On an Island Surrounded by Water (stories and poems)

ALLEY OF THE DOLLS

Science Fiction Stories

Christopher McMaster

Southern Skies Publications

ISBN: 978-1-7385965-5-3 (print)

978-1-7385965-6-0 (eBook)

www.southernskiespublications.com

Cover: Vila Design

For Andrew, a very good friend

contents

ABOVe MY HaLF OF THe WORLD

I t is a small cabin. No surprise there. These old Kazakh miners weren't built for comfort. And it was no doubt purchased second hand from mother Russia, or even the Vietnamese Space Agency. Half a century ago at least. That information is all in the paper work and I could look it up if I cared enough. I don't. I am here for one thing only.

I secure the black case containing computer, communication device and other essential tools on the top bunk and input the code to open it. I withdraw the standard issue pistol, examine the clip and test the safety. I place it in my pocket. Its bulk will be noticeable to any looking, which is what I want.

I start to stow my cap but think twice and put it back on. A hat on a spaceship is stupid, but first impressions count, and the last thing I want them to think is I am their *droog* or *brat*. I'm not their friend or brother, or here to be liked. They're busy with preparations so it's the best time to interrupt. I float out of the cabin and down a narrow corridor, grasp the ladder and propel myself upwards with practiced efficiency.

The captain notices me quietly drift in. He glances briefly and returns to his conversation with an underling. Not a good start. I use a handhold and force my body perpendicular. In zero gravity I could hang upsidedown and it would be the same, but that's not the look I want to convey.

"Captain Omarov," I interrupt.

He stops his interaction and turns. He should have done this the moment he knew I was on the bridge instead of act out some childish display of authority.

"Comrade Komissar," he says, round brown face breaking into a grin. "Welcome to the *Astrograd*. I trust your quarters are comfortable?"

"Neither of us are here to be comfortable, Comrade Captain." I keep my expression emotionless. I have studied his file. He will respond best if he is sure of his standing in professional situations. I want to make it clear where he stands.

"Very true, Comrade Komissar," he replies. "We are honored to have you on board. Have you been to the belt before?"

The usual questions, inquiring about experience. When did you receive your commission? How far out have you travelled? What other deep space vessels have you observed? Sniffing my ass as if we were mutts meeting on the street. I ignore it.

"My priority for this trip is the political wellbeing of all working on the *Astrograd*, including yourself. As a representative of the People's Soviet of Primary Resources, I will also be examining all extraction and processing data. I will require access to pertinent records relating to such during all mining operations."

"Certainly, Comrade Komissar." I note a slight twitch in the corner of his mouth that belies a tell. He understands the hierarchy. Good. He recovers quickly and a grin again fills his face. "I will have First Mate Akhmetov show you our systems which you can access at any time."

"Thank you, Captain," I reply. "That will not be necessary until we reach the Belt and mining commences. I will let you continue with your preparations. Notify me prior to acceleration." I will let you. The sentence isn't lost on the captain. There is another slight twitch in the corner of his mouth.

Again, he recovers quickly. "Certainly, Comrade Komissar."

I turn and with a flick of my wrist descend back down the hatch and return to my cabin. I take the pistol out of my pocket and place it back in the case. It wouldn't help much if the captain and his crew decided to dispose of me, but it might make them think twice. And that hesitation could save my life. Or prolong it, which would be a generous ask.

I lock the door of the cabin behind me. The captain no doubt has master keys, so I search for an internal latch and find it. It was possibly put on by the previous komissar, or even before her. It would merely delay a forced entry, but give enough time to transmit a message. I open my case and take out a monitor to sweep the room. I scan each wall, around my bunk, in every cupboard. I check the vents, popping off covers to allow a visual. The room is clean of any surveillance device.

Now I disassemble the room. There are two questions: where would she hide something she wanted to be found? And where would she hide something she wanted *me* to find? She knew I, and no other komissar, would follow.

The room has two bunks, one on top of the other. It may have been a shared cabin in a past age, but not once komissars have been assigned to the vessel. Komissars are not expected to share rooms. The current use of the top is a storage shelf above the sleeping bunk. I release the restraining net and move my case and personal bag. The bottom is smooth steel, welded to the frame. I pry at each corner, find it is secure, and restow my gear.

I empty the box shelf at the end of the top bunk. There are out of date manuals and old copies of *Krokodil*, *Sovetskaya Kultura* and *Sputnik*. Desperate reading. I am sure I will turn to them in the months to come. I leaf through each page and find nothing.

The bunk below contains a squab, a thin mat for sleeping. I lift it and search beneath, but there is nothing loose and the surface underneath is secure. The squab itself has no disturbed seams and there is no need to cut it open.

The desk is built into the wall beside the bunks. A cabinet is mounted above it, and I start there. There are a few packages of snacks. Her sweet tooth. It makes her soft around the edges, which adds to her beauty. The packets are sealed and I leave them that way. Under them is a first aide case and I dissemble it, careful to keep the contents from floating about the room. I find nothing. Notes are stuck to the back of the cabinet that read like prompts for lectures on patriotism and collectivization. I remove them and examine their backs for any writing, but they are blank.

The surface of the desk is fixed. I run the point of a knife along each edge. The weld is uninterrupted. I open the drawer and find scraps of paper and an old-fashioned watch, with printed numerals and arms indicating hours and minutes. It is unwound and unmoving. I put the watch on so it does not drift off. The papers give me nothing. Bureaucratic forms seldom used. A blank notepad. A roll of adhesive tape. A novel by a banned author. Interesting to find it in the cabin. But who doesn't have a book by a banned author? It is one I have already read. I remove the entire drawer and stow it for the moment on the top bunk. My fingers explore the underside of the desk and I am disappointed when I do not discover a secret panel.

I put the drawer back and focus on the one wardrobe in the cabin. It stretches from floor to ceiling, which means it is a mere four fingers taller than myself. Each shelf within is empty save one. On it are vacuum packed bags containing bed linen. The are sealed, but I open each and unfold them, one by one. They drift about the cabin as thin mute ghosts that tell me nothing. I fold them messily and stuff them back into their bags. I examine the top and bottom for a false ceiling or floor. They are fixed. I pull myself into the chair and strap in, staring at the desk in front of me.

Where would she hide something she wanted found?

I notice I am chewing a fingernail and stop, staring at the digit. A faint memory stirs. Chewing gum stuck under a school desk. Or chair. I reach underneath and explore blindly before unstrapping and moving to the floor to study the bottom of the chair. There is a black panel covering screws that affix the legs to the seat. I pry it off and a small envelope drifts out. I quickly grab and open it. The paper within contains a list of figures. Extraction and processing data. My practiced eye is drawn to the discrepancy between ship's figures and those of the komissar's. They are slight, but if consistent over time they would amount to a sizeable siphoning of profit. It is easy to simply turn a blind eye, still more profitable to demand a percentage. Standard practice. It is the Soviet way.

Captain Omarov is no doubt trying to work out what type of komissar I am. Ignore, profit, or report? I could easily change figures before I submit my data, hiding both of our percentages. It is easy

enough to do. I could equally just report his profiteering. Let him
sweat while he wonders. I do not know his angle, his part in any of
this. Similarly, he does not know mine.

A komissar was not assigned to the *Astrograd's* last trip to the Belt.
And yet I know she boarded the vessel. All that is known on Mars is
that Comrade Komissar Sofiya Vinogradova disappeared from Vostok
Residential Dome 18. Neighbors reported her demeanor different
than usual. Low. Distracted and morose. Everybody is distracted and
morose in Vostok. Officials suspect she left the dome, wandered away
from the settlement and took her own life. It is common, and easy
enough to do in such a hostile environment. Simply admire the view
and open your face mask. I push the image out of my mind. I refuse
to believe that scenario, though I said nothing to dissuade the militsya
from thinking it true, and they close the case.

I run my eye over the data again. She wanted this to be found, so
it may be important. I file it in my black case. But what do you want
me to find? I am chewing my cuticles again. It is a disgusting habit,
but I am incapable of stopping. Or I don't care enough to stop. I
look at my moist fingertip and let my gaze flow from my finger to my
wrinkled palm and then to my wrist. I unclasp the watch and hold
in front of me. It is an admirable piece of work, an antique. I have
always admired old time pieces. An imprint on the back indicates a
well-known workshop in Leningrad. Rare. Valuable.

I raise the timepiece and smash it on the desk top. The glass face
cracks. I smash it again and the back comes loose, offering a glimpse
of the mystery within. I pry open the casing and see a memory chip
wedged in the clockwork gears. Now I am careful. I open my case
stowed on the bunk above and remove a small tool kit. With a pair of
tweezers I remove the chip. It is a simple semi-conductor and looks as

if it were crafted by hand. With a simple attachment I will be able to read the contents on my computer.

Another breadcrumb on the path. What have you left me, Comrade Komissar Sofi?

I am interrupted by an alarm and secure the cabin. I propel myself out of the room and to the acceleration couches. I am assisted in securing my safety straps by the first mate and Omarov comes by with sedatives administered by syringe. I have no choice but to trust him. At this stage I am still untouchable. Only a fool bent on living the rest of their miserable life on a gulag on Ganymede would interfere with a government official in such an obvious situation.

I meet the captain's eye as he injects the drug into my arm. He smiles as he moves to the occupant of the next chair and I feel a numbness spread throughout my body. My gaze drifts to the viewscreen and the red planet below. The lights of Vostok twinkle among the craters. The oldest base on the planet, a stinking cesspit I am only too glad to leave behind, even if I may not live long enough to return. It is the crowning jewel of the Soviet Socialist conquest of space. *Mars is Red!* I mumble the clever slogan and manage to retain a laugh. My mind is growing foggy as the drug takes effect. The weight of acceleration presses me into the seat and shoves my mind to a dark place. The planet fades from my vision as I lose consciousness.

I wake feeling rested and light. The drug has a pleasant side effect that makes my body tingle. And as acceleration is complete, we are back to weightlessness. We are two months away and I will have to be diligent with my physical fitness or I will be as weak as a child by the time we get there. The *Astrograd* is returning to a profitable mine, the People's Soviet of Primary Resources determined to empty the asteroid of every mineral worth taking. Ceres is a large rock, one of the few divided and shared with another power. The other half is mined by the Americans. A trade agreement made during a periodic détente, still in place because a rock orbiting somewhere between Mars and Jupiter is not worth a war. Both are hollowing the planetoid as fast as possible, because wars do happen and profits must not be interrupted. For the crew of the *Astrograd* it is just another run to a very familiar place along a well traversed course.

I am following her every step.

The first mate, Akhmetov, is handing out sachets of water and I take one, greedily sucking it dry. He hands me another before I need to ask and I empty it, leaving the two crumpled containers floating above my chair. At the control station I examine the navigational readings and jot coordinates in a small notebook. The are meaningless, mere show. I could simply make squiggles on the paper as long as they think I notice and note.

After a few more minutes of looking over instrument panels I return to my quarters. The sliver of clear adhesive tape I placed on the seam of the door is unbroken. The room has not been disturbed. I lift the squab, pinch open the small cut I made and withdraw the memory chip. In the black case on the top bunk are the parts needed and I soon attach a link and insert it into my computer. Its contents are encrypted, but it does not take long to decipher. A short passage of writing appears on the screen. At first, it looks like nonsense. Then I remember, evenings reading poetry, before Mars, before Vostok, when we were younger, when we expected so much more …

I read the passage slowly.

we are branded with russia by a white-hot blizzard only how are we to leave each other in our infinite whirling i will live and survive and be asked how they slammed my head against a trestle how i had to freeze at nights how my hair started to turn grey but i'll smile and will crack some

joke and brush away the encroaching shadow and i will render homage
to the dry september that became my second birth i was never tempted
by any other road i mustered strength for all farewells to withstand not
to falter at the last stroke fly away i cannot bear to say farewell yours is
another sky with other laws above my half of the world the comets spread
their tails

There is no punctuation. It is jumbled, bits and pieces from a collection by a dissident poet long before our time, written in a gulag, or memorized or carved into a bar of soap until paper could be obtained. We thought it was romantic to read such works, sheltered by blanket and bathed in candlelight, a secret shared, away from the collective, two alone in the world. I recognize Sofi's favorite line: *And I will render homage to the dry September.* The poet, Irena Ratushinskaya, writes of her unexpected release from the prison.

September is an Earth date, holding no meaning away from the planet. I compute the month into the Mars calendar, review the shipping schedule of the *Astrograd*, its last operation on Ceres. Mining concluded in what would have been the month of September on Earth. *My second birth.* And she musters strength for all farewells, though none were spoken on Vostok. I was deep space when she disappeared, returning to an empty domicile. Sofi has left me a goodbye. But like the data from under the chair, it hides more, only seen by one who can understand. *I cannot bear to say farewell. Yours is another sky. Fly away.*

Its hidden message invades my sleep and I dream of her beside me. Then she wakes and leaves our bed, padding naked to the door. There she stops and turns, lifts a hand to me and beckons with a bent finger.

Weeks slowly pass in a blur of routine. The sameness of each day makes one blend into another until I am surprised time passes at all. I spend three hours physical training, trying to maintain muscle mass. It is a losing battle. In the hold, I inspect each harvester that will be deployed in the mines. The software controlling the machines has safeguards against tampering but they are easily overridden. If you know how. I organize history and political lessons for the crew. These are not optional. It is for my own diversion. I take a mild satisfaction in making the crew squirm, and I actually enjoy the subject.

"And why, Comrades, do we owe so much to the mind of Comrade Mikhail Bakhtin?" I pierce a miner in the front row with my eyes. He flinches, purses his mouth as he burrows through distant memories of school for any recollection. I let him suffer several moments before putting him out of his misery.

"Exactly," I say. "Just what you are doing now. Thinking. Or trying to, at least." Laughter ripples through the room. "And he taught us about *being*. 'Because I am actual and irreplaceable, I must actualize my uniqueness.' His words. What do you think he saying? Never mind, Comrade, we haven't all day." More laughter. "He reminds us that it is the duty, no, the obligation, of every Soviet citizen to perform to the highest moral and ethical standard for the betterment of not just themselves, but of all citizens."

There are some nods as the miners agree, or pretend to. "And sticking with old men with beards, what can you tell me of Kropotkin? Peter Kropotkin. He is why you are here, working on this little self-governing community at the farthest reaches of the Union *actualizing* yourselves. The principle of the worker-run enterprise ..." And on and on. I reluctantly grow to look forward to these meetings, even if my students would rather be sleeping or drinking vodka. They are my captive audience and I indulge myself.

Finally, the time for deceleration arrives. The great ship has turned and faces away from Ceres as its engines prepare to fire again, this time slowing our momentum. I sit in the couch and offer my arm to Omarov, captain and ship medic. There is no red planet out the window to stare at this time, only the black emptiness of a cold and vicious space. No lights flash by like in the movies at the cinema, ships speeding across the vast expanse. There is nothing but black. The numbness brings its own kind of darkness. I fall into it.

Mining continues for weeks. I go to the bridge for every harvest. I check returning diggers disgorging their haul. I am in the factory as valuable minerals are extracted from the ore. I watch as the useless slag is ejected onto the surface of the asteroid, creating new geological formations on the lifeless mini-world. I input the data into my programs. It is very easy to see where Omarov is skimming. How he turns that into profit and where he hides it are interesting questions, but I don't care enough to investigate. I hide his profiteering with a simple sleight of hand, so to speak—I am no magician. The data is simple to manipulate. Only a very skilled forensic analyst would notice, and few such analysts work for the People's Soviet of Primary Resources. Sofi was a good analyst. What deal did she make with the captain?

Mining is nearing its end and it is time to call a meeting with Omarov. I choose the mess room as it offers more privacy, but there are cameras everywhere and I am sure we will be keenly watched. I deliberatively sit with my back to the door, placing myself in a vulnerable position. Omarov sits across from me, wearing a grin that is false. I have spent weeks degrading the man while I assess the situation and decide my next move. A captain and a komissar are equivalent rank. But I have not interfered or overridden any of his orders or decisions during the operation. I could have. It was within my authority, but I didn't. It may slow his hand. That is my one card to play. I lay it on the table.

"You have been siphoning what belongs to the people for your personal gain," I say.

Omarov's grin flattens and he stares at me. I feel a presence at my back, a crew member at the mess hatchway.

"The penalty for profiteering is not the gulag. It is death." I do not have long before the conversation is cut short by the crew member behind me and whatever weapon he holds.

"I can teach you how to hide your activities better," I add. "I am a better analyst than Comrade Komissar Sofiya Vinogradova."

His expression remains flat but I am still alive. Then I say: "You must have found her a very special woman."

Omarov is momentarily confused, a new tell, in the eyebrows. He recovers quickly.

"Show Akhmetov your trick," he says. "He has a much better mind for such things. And yes, I found her a very unique woman."

We sit staring at each other as a moment passes, followed by another.

"There is a note in my cabin," I tell him. "It is a sad story, of a lonely komissar far from home who lost his lover. He has no reason to live, so he decides to end his life."

Omarov has recovered his grin. I have given him his power back and I wait to see how he uses it. There is no more hierarchy. I am totally defenseless. He raises a finger and I wait for it fall. But he speaks instead.

"Vodka!"

The shape behind me moves closer and proffers sachets of the alcohol to myself and the captain. We touch them as a toast and I drink with Omarov.

"She was certainly worth dying for, comrade," he says. "A real beauty."

I turn and watch the *Astrograd* leave the surface, returning to Mars, belly full. I have eight hours of oxygen. I walk towards the opposite side of the asteroid. My air will not last the time it takes to cross to the American side, but I will issue a distress call before then. They will rush to rescue a defector, as she knew. I scan the surface as I walk, large looping strides in the light gravity, covering several meters with each step. After some distance I see a print left in the dust, and another, leading away, towards the foreign station. The outline of the boot can only be hers. I stop and bend to touch one with gloved finger.

And then I stand and look up, expecting to see comets spread their tails.

Mack the Hack

J ake McKenna sat in his car sipping tepid coffee. He was surprised it had any warmth at all. He bought it with a breakfast burrito from a gas station what must have been hours ago. Time didn't improve the taste of the drink, even if it was still lukewarm. He rolled his window down a few more inches than it already was and poured the rest of the coffee onto road. The passenger seat beside him held a camera that was worth more than the car. A note pad sat on the dash, and the floor was covered in the detritus of too many hours of occupancy. Empty paper coffee cups, scrunched up food wrappers from a variety of fast-food outlets, a half-eaten stale donut.

Jake McKenna made a wry grin and shook his head. It finally happened. He had become a cliché. Mack the Hack. That was the kind of name that sticks, and he'd been called it before. That was when he worked for the *Journal*. God, what a rag. He worked it because he needed a regular paying job and in journalism those were few and far between. Everybody at the *Journal* was a hack, and he told the editor that at his 'leaving interview.' What they did wasn't journalism. They just cared about an undefined bottom line, making as much money for the shareholders as possible through sensationalized tripe. Turn everything into a drama, create a crisis out of a cup cake.

He knew that when he started to think in dramatic headlines that it was finally time to leave. Slip in the shower and almost fall? Bathroom Horror! Domestic Routine Results in Near Death. Cut off by another driver on the way to work? Highway Mayhem! Drivers Lose Control on City Streets! He could even write one about the donut on the floor. A couple weeks ago, he probably would.

"By printing this stuff you're cheapening what we do," he told the editor. "This isn't journalism. It's just bad entertainment. No, it's not even that. It's naked sensationalism. How many times can you use 'shock' and 'horror' in your headlines? It's a race to the bottom, and you're leading the charge." He laid it on thick.

"Well, we'll just have to agree to disagree." She wasn't subtle as she looked at her watch. The interview was over.

Mack wanted to exit with a few choice names thrown her way. Instead, he left her office and went to a bar. After three drinks he felt his pulse regain a somewhat normal rhythm. He asked for a glass of water and nursed it as if it were much stronger. He pulled out the small notepad he always carried and read what he jotted on the first pages. It wasn't much. But it was a lead, he was certain of that. He had a nose for leads, even if most didn't take him anywhere. He didn't bring this one to an editor, especially the one at the *Journal*. There was no investigative journalism there.

That's what he always wanted to do. It took too many months to realize that to actually do that he had to be unemployed. Scratch that. The unemployed don't keep the kind of hours he was putting in. No, he was freelance. He didn't have a contract, or even a paper or magazine he intended to submit to. But when he finished there'd be plenty who'd want it. He was certain of that. Just as long as his savings didn't run out before he finished the story, or at least had enough to interest the right platform to keep funding him.

His small notepad had more writing in it after so many days spent in his car. The first notes were brief, a few words and a small sketch of a large warehouse. He was covering a story for the *Journal*, he couldn't remember what that was about, when he first noticed the place. It was toward the industrial part of the city, so may have been a work place accident or a drug overdose or any other kind of catastrophe that was yet another example of society falling apart. Shock. Horror. He added to the sketch since. A large tall chain link fence surrounded the building, topped with razor wire. A large gate was set into the fence was the only entrance. A guard both stood at the gate, and was always occupied, whatever the time of day or night. Mack knew this because he drove by at different times of the day and night. Not enough to draw attention to his vehicle, but enough to confirm.

He picked up his camera when a bus passed. His watch read the same time as it did yesterday when it went by. There wasn't a lot of traffic at the complex. His notes recorded the arrival of a goods truck on several occasions, like the bus, keeping to regular schedule. The guard checked the driver's identification and let it pass. Mack tried to find a position where he could see it park or unload, but it entered a large roller door, and the door closed behind it. The only other time he saw it was when it was driving away. Presumably empty. Or presumably full. He drew a question mark in his pad. At different times an ambulance arrived at the gate and was waved through after the usual check. It arrived at no set times. It left again shortly later. Mack recorded its stay: twelve minutes, eighteen minutes, ten minutes. A pick-up? A drop off? Mack didn't know. Another question mark. The ambulance didn't have a company or hospital name emblazoned on its side. It didn't have any writing at all, but it was still an ambulance.

He took a picture of the bus as it stopped at the gate. The guard climbed aboard and exited minutes later. Mack took more pictures, even though he had plenty, zoomed close to show the guard conducting a head count and writing on his clip board. Mack concluded that the bus ferried workers to the warehouse. In twenty minutes it would exit, as it did every day, full of workers at the end of their shift. It did this every eight hours, around the clock. Mack followed the bus for the previous two days. He took pictures of workers disembarking. They looked like normal working-class men and women, finishing up a day at work.

He chose a woman to follow each time, selecting one around his age. He thought he was lucky yesterday. She walked a mere block away from the bus and down a street reflecting the economic status of somebody who worked in a large white warehouse behind a tall fence. Not the best neighborhood. She turned up the path to a small house, one a single woman might live in. Before she could get her keys out the door opened and two little kids mobbed her. She ruffled a little boy's hair and hugged who Mack assumed was his sister before they all went inside and closed the door. He strolled past the house picking his teeth and walked around the entire block to get back to his car without having to pass the house twice.

He knew from experience that if you wanted information, you had to ask the right person. The right kind of person. Mack found her on the third try. She got off the bus closer to an apartment complex, the type you don't want to live in if you could help it. He pulled over on the side of the road and turned off the engine. He used the zoom on the camera to watch her climb to the second level, a terrace right above the ground floor. She passed several doors before opening one and closing it behind her. He hid the camera under the rubbish on the floor and was about to step out and lock the car behind him, go to her door and give it a knock, when it opened and she stepped back onto the terrace. He fumbled for the camera and focused the lens. She had changed into blue jeans and light blouse. Her brown hair was loose. She was quite pretty, in a tired way, but she had just completed an eight-hour shift. Mack watched as she descended the stairs and crossed the parking lot to a bar that sat right next to the complex.

He couldn't believe his luck. He stashed the camera again, locked the car and crossed the road. He waited outside the bar for several minutes before going inside. It was run of the mill run down, a dark place to drink. He stood just inside the door temporarily blinded by the gloom. His eyes adjusted and he searched the room. Small tables lined a wall, a long bar stood opposite. She was perched on a stool two-thirds of the way down nursing what looked like a gin and tonic. The two stools next to her were empty. That meant she wasn't here with anybody. He sat at the second one and ordered a beer, took a long draught before turning towards her.

"Always a nice time of the day," Mack said.

She looked at him. He didn't look like a creep. But the jury was still out.

"Off the clock. Free time. No gods, no masters."

"I can drink to that," she said, and she did.

Mack took another mouthful, swallowed. "I'm Jake," he said, offering a hand. "But folks call me Mack."

She took his hand, shook it briefly. "Nice to meet you, Mack. I'm Julie."

He drew a blank on what to say next that didn't sound creepy, so he told a joke about a bear that went into a bar and ordered a rum and a … coke. Why the big pause? The bartender asks, and the bear holds up his paws and says he didn't know, he always had them. Not as corny as the horse with the long face, but she laughed. She told one of her own.

When her drink got low Mack ordered a round. He didn't ask about her work until a full hour had passed, casual, just curious. He had a story about being a quality control supervisor in a food processing plant not very far from there, inspecting tomatoes. They were grown in the area. In case she asked him to reciprocate. She never did.

"I'm in healthcare," she answered.

"Are you a nurse?"

"If I were a nurse I wouldn't be working where I do." She turned back to her drink.

"One of those jobs where you're on your feet all day?"

"Boy, you got that right." She nodded.

"So what do you do in this healthcare job?" Mack asked. He was pushing. But that's why he was there.

She shook her head, staring at her drink. "Can't tell you."

"A lady of mystery. Now I'm curious."

"Seriously," she said. "It's in my employment contract. Non-disclosure clause. We're reminded of it frequently. I'd have to kill you if I told."

"Or they'd kill you?"

Mack smiled at his flippant remark. Her eyes grew wide for a second but she recovered quickly. Mack drank the rest of the beer in his glass and pretended nothing happened. But it was clear she didn't want to talk about work anymore.

"Hey," he said. "These make a mighty fine dinner but I could use something I can chew. What do you say we grab a bite around the corner before coming back here for more? My treat. I'm the hungry one."

"I'm hungry too," she said. "But you can still pay."

She had a burger and fries and he settled on a steak, and when they finished the meal, they skipped desert and went back to the bar. After another few drinks she decided that he could follow her home and depending on how he performed, maybe even spend the night. A girl had needs. She fell asleep after the second time and Mack lay in bed beside her. Part of him wanted to slip out of the covers, grab his clothes and sneak out, back to his car and his own apartment. Another part wanted to stay put. He didn't know if it was the journalist or the man who enjoyed this woman's company that wanted to stay or leave.

Mack put his hands behind his head and stared at the ceiling, pretending that he wasn't a total scoundrel. He ran through everything she said about her work. It wasn't much. Beside it being in healthcare, which he already suspected, she didn't say anything. Because she couldn't. And that was actually something. Whatever was going on inside the warehouse somebody didn't want the outside world knowing about. So much so they made their employees sign non-disclosure agreements with a possible unpleasant consequence if they did. Was that really so unusual in industry nowadays? He played back her response in the bar. She was scared of something.

Julie's alarm woke both of them. He thought she looked pretty in the morning, but she ignored his touches and climbed out of bed, padded to the bathroom and started the shower. She closed the door behind her, so Mack got out of bed and dressed. He ran a finger across his teeth. He'd have to run to his own place and clean up a bit if he got the chance. He knew he wouldn't, or even feel the need, once he was back in his car. A gas station bathroom would do. The shower was still running, so he moved quickly.

He looked around Julie's place. There was little to make it personal. A few books. She was evidently into historical romance. A cheap print depicting a tropical island that may have come with the place hung on the wall. A framed photo of a small girl and a dog. Maybe she had a kid, maybe it was a sister, or even her quite a few years ago. The kitchenette had the basics for making small meals. He rifled her purse. Her wallet held some cash, a credit card, a driver's license. Julie Anne Ennis. She was older than he guessed, but not a lot more. A key chain with a bobble attached. Apartment key, car key, one that looked like it was a for a pad lock. No keys or fobs that looked work related. No work identification or pass.

Would her bank account show deposits from her employer? Maybe, but he didn't have the skill to hack into an account, and strongly suspected payments wouldn't show depositor details. He was looking at the credit card when he realized the room was quiet. The shower had stopped. He put the card back in Julie's wallet, wallet back in the purse and purse back on the counter. He poured a glass of water and started to drink at the same time the bathroom door opened.

"Mind if I use that room?" he asked as she walked out.

"Only if you're quick," she said.

"No problem there," he answered.

He entered, had a quick piss and a glance in her medicine cabinet (band-aids, birth control pills, aspirin and not much else), flushed the toilet and washed his hands. She was dressed and by the door when he came out.

"You look nice. Casual dress at work?" he asked.

"Only wear scrubs there," she said, holding the door open. She bit her lip, then smiled. "Thanks for the night, but now you gotta go, buster."

He stepped outside and she closed and locked the door behind them. Julie hustled down the stairs and Mack hurried to catch up. He stopped her at the bottom and gave her a quick kiss.

"See you again?"

"I'll be around," she answered before striding across the parking lot to the bus stop. It pulled up the same time she got there. She climbed in and disappeared.

Mack waited until the bus was out of sight before crossing the street to his car. He scribbled notes in his pad, everything he could recall that Julie said, and some of what she didn't. He wrote the word 'scrubs'. You don't wear scrubs if you work on an assembly line. Or did you? Mack thought they were for working with people, but he wasn't sure.

He parked in a different location near the warehouse and continued his surveillance. When an ambulance arrived, he pulled a U-turn and followed as it left. It drove passed the nearest hospital, continued north east, and eventually stopped at a private clinic. Mack took pictures as the driver got out, opened the back of the truck and withdrew a plastic cooler. He zoomed close and snapped a pic of the dial on the lid. Somebody was receiving a delicate specimen. Like a blood sample. Viral swabs. Some type of medicine. Or a body part.

Mack followed the ambulance back to a small depot. It pulled into a garage that housed another unlabeled ambulance. The door closed behind, sealing them in their garage. The driver didn't re-emerge. The second time he followed one of the ambulances it went to the same clinic (always the same private clinic). He almost dropped his camera. The driver got out, as before, went to the back, opened the door and lifted out a carrier with a baby inside. Mack refocused and zoomed close enough to catch the little thing's eyes. He waited for mom step out, but the driver just closed the back and went into the clinic.

He followed the goods truck to its terminal. He watched through his lens as it prepared for its next run to the factory, took pictures as cleaning supplies and food stuffs were loaded on. It was a lot cleaning supplies and food stuffs. He made tallies in his notepad and studied the list after the truck left on its way to the warehouse.

The second time he saw Julie he showed up at her apartment with takeaway. She liked burgers so he brought some with fries and soda.

"How did you know I was home?" she asked.

"Lucky guess. And you weren't in the bar."

She deflected any questions he had about her work, even when they weren't questions. She made it clear that she wasn't going to talk about that topic with him, without having to say anything about not talking about the topic. But when she left in the morning he noticed she didn't pack a lunch.

"No lunch? Hope they feed you well at that work place of yours," he said.

"It's passable," was all she offered.

Mack scanned the list in his pad. It didn't compute. There was far too much food going into the place. He continued to watch the terminal. Other trucks came, loaded, and went. One person sat in the small office. He used the zoom lens to look closely at the eaves, or any other place a camera might be mounted. Unlike the tall fence and guard at the warehouse, or the shuttered ambulance depot, the place seemed lightly protected. He scanned through some of the pictures he took of the workers and bought a close match to their tan work pants and blue shirt-sleeve work shirt they wore.

The night before he went in, he paid Julie a visit. He didn't think he got much from her to help his story, but he liked her company. When he found out more, he could be more direct. Honest. They went to the bar but he stopped after two drinks because he knew he couldn't keep up with her and didn't want a hangover in the morning. Even full of drink she gave nothing about her work, talking about growing up in Indiana and a dog she was crazy about when she was a girl. Yeah, that was her in the photo. She passed out right after sex and woke up grumpy. Her mood improved when Mack dashed out during her shower and bought her a breakfast burrito. She was still eating it as she climbed aboard her bus.

Mack looked at his watch and hurried to his car. He changed his clothes in the front seat, stashed his wallet and note pad in the glove box and drove to the truck terminal. He looked at the camera!. Too bulky. He hid it under the garbage on the floor, pocketed his phone and walked to the trucks. This part wasn't difficult. It was all timing. He hung back by the road, watched two men begin to load the truck. When they went back inside for more supplies, Mack walked to the back of the truck, jumped inside and with some quick rearranging, hid behind the stack of boxes. He was soon concealed by a wall of more. The roller door at the back of the truck rattled down and he stood in the darkness. The truck jerked as it pulled away. Mack grabbed hold of the wall to steady himself, tightened his grip as the truck turned into traffic.

Time seemed to slow as they drove towards the warehouse, but Mack knew how long it took. He glanced at his watch but couldn't see dial or numbers. He was as blind as he was flying at the moment. He took a deep breath and tried not to shudder as he exhaled. He needed ice in his veins. He inhaled slowly through his nostrils and exhaled. That was better. Mack bumped a box when they stopped at the gate. It fell and made a sound that sounded like a car crash to Mack. He waited for the back to open and to be hauled out, but the truck lurched again as it pulled into the complex. He held onto the wall as he felt it slow, tilt up the slight slope into the warehouse, and jerk to a stop.

The rollup door at the back of truck began to rise and Mack squatted behind boxes. The men began unloading, taking a box each and carrying it away. When they ate into the barrier hiding Mack, he waited for them to carry their next away, picked a box and climbed out of truck behind them. Tall shelves full of supplies stood under a high ceiling. The two workers from the truck disappeared with their boxes down an aisle and Mack took his to the closest row of shelves. He set the box on one and moved further down the aisle, past stacks of toilet paper, containers of soaps and shampoos, containers of laundry detergents, hiding in a canyon of toiletries. Mack withdrew his phone, opened the camera app and took several pictures. He stood at the end of the aisle, able to duck in the one he came from or the aisle adjacent and keep out of sight. He didn't have to. The men finished unloading and the truck started, the door to the warehouse slid open and clanked shut after the vehicle had left.

Mack waited and listened. An eerie silence filled the vast space. Camera in hand, he moved cautiously to the next aisle, and then another, further into the storage room. Walls that did not reach the ceiling partitioned the area from the rest of the vast building. Doors led away to other rooms. Each had a label, and a warning. Authorized Personnel Only. He opened the door with Laundry Services mounted on a sign above it with an icon depicting a washing machine. Mack took pictures of unattended washing and drying machines humming through their programs. Industrial size machines. The type a large hotel would have. Mack opened a drier and felt damp bedding inside. He closed the door and restarted the machine. He opened another and was hit by a wave of hot air. Reaching in, he withdrew warm grey scrubs. Mack took off his brown pants and blue shirt, rolled them up into a tight wad and dumped them in a nearby trash can. He put on the scrubs and slid his phone in a wide pocket.

Opening the door to Laundry Services, Mack slipped out of the room. Walking close to the wall he headed to another marked Food Services. Icon of a pot with a ladle in it. The door opened before he reached it and a woman wearing grey scrubs emerged. She glanced at him, nodded once, and continued down a storage aisle stacked with boxes of foods. Mack was glad he didn't have time for a second coffee in the morning and his bladder was relatively empty. He inhaled slowly as he continued forward, exhaling and willing his heart to slow to something closer to a normal rhythm. He reached for a door with Dormitory and a picture of a bed above. It opened to a short hallway that ended in another door with the same label. Mack opened it just enough to peer through, and then a bit more to allow his body through.

He took a quick picture of rows of single beds stretching across the room and slipped his phone back in his pocket. Each bed was exactly the same, white metal frame, white sheets, thin white blankets. The room was open and exposed. It had the same eerie silence of the storage room. But this room was not completely empty. Men and women wearing grey scrubs moved about, straightening bedcovers or picking up white gowns dropped on the floor. There were no boxes or shelves to hide behind, just row upon row of beds. He looked at the door he came through. A safe retreat. He inhaled and took a step into the room, and then another. He kept breathing calmly, trying to maintain a phony calm. He stooped and ran his hand over a bed, copying the motions of the others as they straightened covers.

Mack scanned their faces for Julie's, pleased he didn't see it. He continued across the room in the direction of another door, an escape from the Dormitory. He aimed for one labelled Nutrition. A plate and utensils icon. A man in scrubs stepped in front of him, quickly moved and made a circular motion with his fist over his heart. He nodded briefly and moved past, picking up a white gown from the floor. Mack watched him pick up yet another and add it to the bundle in his arms. Mack pretended to straighten another bed before reaching the door. He opened it and entered a room full of men and women sitting at tables eating. The only sounds in the room were of spoons or forks clicking on metal trays, the scrape of chairs being moved, or empty trays being set on a counter to be collected by people in grey scrubs.

He watched a woman in a white gown spoon what looked like scrambled eggs into her mouth, chew and swallow, lift a piece of toast and take a bit. He placed her around mid-twenties. Blond hair. Pale complexion. Aside from a gauze bandage on the inside of her arm, she looked healthy. Mack focused on another woman. Mid-Twenties, blond hair, pale skin. She sat slightly back from the table to make room for her swollen belly. She was very pregnant. Another woman at the table finished her breakfast and rose to take her empty tray to the counter. Youngish, mid-twenties, blond hair, pale skin. Mack clamped his jaw tight to stop a gasp from escaping. He was looking at the same woman. Every woman was the same.

It itched where Mack's camera touched his leg through the scrub's pocket, but he resisted the urge to scratch. To take out his phone and record what he saw. He watched as the woman deposited her empty tray and entered a doorway with Ablutions and a picture of hands and bubbles above it. Then Mack looked at a man in a white gown. Mid-twenties. Brown hair. Pale skin. He expected what he saw when he shifted his gaze to another. The same man, sitting in a different chair, eating a different breakfast. Like the women, some wore bandages and some did not. Some moved gingerly as if they carried an injury.

Mack continued across the dining room towards a door with Clinic written above it, and an icon with a red cross beside it. He opened the door and entered, breathing easier as the room was close to empty. Close. A woman in her mid-twenties, with blond hair and pale skin, was strapped to an examination chair. Her arms and feet immobilized. A clear plastic bag sat next to one foot, slowly filling with blood. Mack followed the tube from the bag as it led to the woman's arm. He stepped over to her.

"Are you okay?" he asked. "Do you want this?"

The woman furled her brow and frowned. She could not use her hands so communicated the only way she knew. She did not understand what the Attendant wanted because he did not communicate. He only made strange sounds form his mouth.

"I can get you out of here," he promised. "Here, wait a sec." The itch had grown too great and Mack removed his phone and took several pictures before putting it back.

"Let me undo these for you," he said, bending and unstrapping her arms and legs. He un-taped the needle in her arm and gently withdrew it.

She stared at him silently, eyes wide, before holding her hand open in front of her chest and vibrating it. You are frightening me, she told him. But Mack didn't understand. He made strange noises again.

"You're okay now, follow me."

She held her open hand in front of her chest again and wiggled it. Mack reached to take her hand and she shrunk away. She made the hand movement again. Then she looked past Mack and relaxed. Mack staggered backwards as a strong hand gripped his scrub and pulled him away from the young woman. He bumped against a body much bigger than his. Hot breath at his ear whispered, a threatening rasp.

"Do not say another word. She has never heard language and you are frightening her."

A woman in grey scrubs stepped past them and gestured to the blond in white. The conversation was lost on Mack. One made a simple sign, followed by the other. The blond sat back in the examination chair. The woman in grey touched her chin with an open hand and lowered it. The blond in white ran her open hand across her mouth. Mack watched as her feet were re-secured, but lost sight of them as he was turned around and pushed through a door marked Clinic Supplies with an icon of a syringe next to the words.

As soon as they were out of the clinic Mack was shoved roughly across a small storeroom. He staggered and fell sprawling on the concrete floor. Before he could regain his feet, his scrub was grabbed again and he was hoisted upright and shoved forward and through an unmarked door at the other side of the small room. As soon as they were through that door he was shoved again, harder. Mack hit the floor and slid forward. He was helped up in the same manner, lifted across the room and deposited on a waiting chair. He felt plastic bite into his arms and ankles as ties secured him to the arms and legs of the chair. Mack stared from where he sat at the first person in the center that he saw not wearing scrubs or a gown.

"We value security here and don't take kindly to those who do not belong," the man in front of him said.

"He spoke to Sixty-Three," a man behind him said.

"That is most unfortunate," the man in front said.

"I'm an investigative reporter for the *Journal*," Mack tried. "My editor knows exactly where I am. If I don't check in with her in one hour, you'll have a lot more people here that don't belong."

The man smiled and withdrew Mack's wallet from a pocket of his expensive suit. He opened and withdrew Mack's driver's license.

"No, Mr. McKenna," he said. "Your editor isn't expecting a call from you. She said you had some kind of breakdown and quit your job at the paper some weeks ago. She didn't seem to like you very much."

He tossed Mack's wallet on the floor and ignored it. "Nobody knows where you are, Mr. McKenna."

He looked above Mack and nodded. Mack heard a rustle behind him and everything went blurry. He fought for breath but the plastic bag placed over his head was sealed tight, held firmly by strong hands. It wasn't long before Mack stopped struggling.

Julie's shift was almost over. Her feet hurt. She was cleaning the ablution stall when a co-worker stood in front of her. He held a hand flat and placed two fingers behind it. It took a while, but she was used to the non-verbal nature of communication at her work. You are wanted at the office. She raised her fingers to her chin and lowered them before returning to the cleaning the basin. Thank you. Her co-worker tapped his wrist. Go now. Julie nodded and they left together.

The manager spoke as soon as she entered the office. "Thank you for coming, Ms. Ennis. Please take a seat." He gestured to a chair immediately in front of his desk.

Julie sat and her co-worker stood behind her. "What is this about?" Julie asked.

"You are well aware of the very strict non-disclosure clause of your employment contract." It was more statement than question.

"Of course I am," Julie said. "I take it very serious. I've never—"

"You've never spoken to a journalist named Jake McKenna?" He held up Mack's driver's license, moving towards her so she could see the image.

"I don't know any—" she started. She peered at the small picture. "Hey, I didn't know he was a journalist. And I didn't tell him anything!"

The man behind the desk pulled out a small note pad taken from Mack's car before it was driven to a wrecker's yard and smashed into a cube of metal. He flicked through several pages before leaving it alone.

"There are things here that he could only know from one of our employees," he said. "You, Ms. Ennis, are that employee." Then he looked above Julie and nodded.

ALLEY OF THE DOLLS

I said hey listen up you punks I got a good one so they did except eric who belched real loud but then he quietened down and listened cause I got real good ideas like rabbit run surprised none of us got killed with that idea that would have ruined the buzz but nobody did good for all of us so we could go back to the room and fall over laughing with relief and snort another line simple that one just start at the edge of the six lane freeway and run to the other side nighttime and traffic trying to stop you dead the smart rabbit stops at the lines in between the lane like one lane at a time takes a little slower but gets to the other side in one piece but a smarter rabbit just cuts loose and sprints timing perfect or lucky stars aligned preferably both had to move down the road a mile or so when a car swerved to miss Chip that would have missed him anyway dumb fuck shouldn't be behind a wheel and hit the car next to it which scrapped against the concrete divider sparks flying and metal grinding

hard to run from that when you're doubled over busting a gut laughing but we all made like a banana and got the fuck out of there good night hard to match but I think I had that problem solved and evidently so did this gang of losers gauging by their gawking eyes and open mouths we're gonna hunt the hookers I told them they all kept staring so I explained some more look I told them I been researching and doing a little experimenting and this is gonna be a sight to behold I said and I pulled out my moms big pink dildo from my backpack which got their attention as I knew it would but I already had their attention it didn't look much like a long fat cock anymore which was the whole point and I had to tell the dumb fuckers what it was just to confirm their suspicions

they finally closed their gaping holes and then opened them again to tell me I was a sick fuck and what was I doing playing with my moms dildo what was I a queer or something but there was nothing wrong with that Chip was probably leaning that way and none of us cared they didn't say that last part I just wanted to make it clear that it was okay to be gay or whatever else you wanted to be who the fuck cares not any of my business and shouldn't be yours

its not what it is its what its made out of I said talking about the dildo but they still said I was a fag so I set the lump of misshapen pink rubber on the coffee table and they all scoot back from it like its going to bite them or crawl up their pants to explore but they were still listening Eric Chip who you already met and Ronnie and Beck the whole crew its TPE you dimwits knowing they wouldn't know what TPE is and I just liking calling them stupid because mostly they were except Chip maybe who could even go to college if he stopped tweaking so much but he didn't know what I was talking about either so I elaborated

look I told them sex toys are made of this shit either this or silicon or rubber or plastic even wood for chrissakes cause folk will fuck or stick anything up their holes but the best is TPE cause its flexible soft as hell its even recyclable called thermoplastic elastomer but TPE for short like MDMA is short for some crazy ass long words which is why we call it Molly so TPE keeps the heat and stays soft which is why its used for dildos and pocket pussies and sex dolls and shit like that seriously I thought Chip would start to twig what I was laying out by then but he was as clueless as the others so I confused them more with some of my useless learning just to fuck with them so I say see its organic even if it don't look like it its the feel that maters in these cases its made out of styrene butadiene styrene rubber polypropylene zinc stearate and some other shit just as if youre wondering I add at the end of my explanation knowing full well they weren't wondering I could see I was gonna loose the audience if I didn't move on to the demo part so I reached into my backpack and took out a glass jar full of my special concoction of dimethyl sulfoxide acetone benzene and a little secret I'll keep and then I unscrewed the top and they scuttled back further whining about the smell

I was surprised they could smell at all with their abused nostrils but evidently they could so I told them to stop being babies and watch and I set the jar down on the table and picked up the dildo giving the munted thing a couple strokes and they busted a laugh and I said what you have before you is a typical ten inch baloney pony speaking as if I were on an infomercial or cooking show and then I set it on the table and picked up the jar and without carrying on like I was on television cause I could see they were about to give up and get up I poured some of my magic juice on the dildo and that got their attention and they all leaned in and watched as the disfigured monstrous cock disfigured even more where I already experimented on it dissolved where the fluid touched it not melting like it was in an oven or anything but literally dissolving the fucking thing leaving a mess underneath on the table whoa said Beck like I knew he would because he loves this kind of shit and Eric says to do more but I says we got to save as much as the shit as possible cause we got a some hunting to do and I tell the plan and then do another line

we stumble out of the apartment and onto a thirty two that took us to the nineteen that dropped us right where we wanted where youd want to be if you wanted a good time with the ladies we passed a few ladies real humans these ones still trying to ply their trade before the new hookers took their jobs but they were in the wrong spot we were looking for a particular alley that was becoming quite popular of late because that's where the new girls hung out youd think itd be easier find but we eventually did and peered down the dark little canyon where the whores and their johns were exchanging money and making grunts and gasps we walked down the narrow lane like johns ourselves on the prowl because in a way we were and I set my eyes the hooker I wanted her pink flesh if you could call it that reflected the faint light in the alley she wore what somebody thought was sexy lingerie and maybe it was id admit if I were being honest black three quarter stockings garter belt crotchless panties and a thin black bra where her nipples peeked through you want a good time she asked and I almost backed down cause I didn't know they could speak these wonders of science and technology and thermoplastic elastomer but the guys were behind me so I had no real choice in the matter anyway it was full speed ahead damn the whatever

she turned slowly as if to display the merchandise bulbous pink butt hiding a small tight hole slit at the front hiding another between round thighs her mouth formed a small o and I pointed at that part of her face and said that and she just like that knelt in front of me and started undoing my pants o of a mouth waiting as soon as I was hard and ready but before she could take my man meat all the way out I placed a hand on her head slid off her wig and poured the whole jar of my serum over her face she didn't shout or cry in pain because they don't feel no pain she just knelt there and her eyes widened until they formed much bigger o's than her mouth until they became big holes in her face and her face ran down taking her small o for a mouth with them and continued its gruesome jaunt to her shoulder and breasts that melted and sagged solution doing its work she looked at me with those eyes that weren't eyes and reached for my pants again inviting me to use her o but all that was there now was her titanium cranium and Im not ashamed to say I freaked a little I backed against the wall and fumbled to fasten my belt and zipper and begin to run but not before the walking talking sex toy asked if I wanted to use her ass side instead

I heard the slap of feet behind me from the gang running almost as fast freaked almost as much down three no four blocks imagining we were chased by the robot sex toy or her pimp but it was just us we caught a nineteen back to a thirty two back to the inner sanctum of Ronnies crappy little apartment and only then did we fall about in relief and exhilaration laughing ourselves sick and sculling back beer trying not to think of her skull and doing lines so wed never sleep and see that gaping o of a mouth it was a long time before I got another good idea like that one but that's another story

Sarge

"I died when I was five or six," Jiao said.

Her squad leaned forward. Sarge didn't talk much about herself. She didn't even smile, at least not that her platoon ever saw. The way her mouth wrinkled at the left corner could never be mistaken for a smile, though it may have displayed an unhealthy indication of enjoyment. It only came out when danger was close.

"I was really sick. All I remember is the sensation of sand grating against sand, like I was a piece of sand paper being turned back against itself, grinding against itself. Yeah, that was it. Me. Leaving my body. I think it was prepping me for this shit."

Jiao closed her eyes and saw her grandmother lean over and carefully place a damp cloth on her forehead. Like the physical sensation of the fever, her grandmother's expression burned into her memory. There was another presence near, her grandfather. It was summer, because she spent every summer at their house. Her mother put her on a flier which took her south to the long island grandfather named Pounamu, with its mountain range running along its spine reminding him of his home on earth. Pounamu was the name of the green gem mined there. Jade. She wore a pendant of it under her uniform.

Snow fell at the higher elevations, but not in the summer. Jiao had never seen snow up close.

Strategically, Pounamu was weak. The Beakers simply pushed the defenders against the heights and picked them off as they tried to clamber over the summit to escape, their desperate thermal images giving them away. Or the invaders just let them starve and freeze in some canyon or crevice, hemmed in by cliffs of crumbling rock. Retreat into a cave, Jiao thought, you deserve what you get. And you will get it. That's why the Beakers have that island now, and why there's a lot of bleached bones in those mountains.

Jiao liked to swim in the sheltered bay in front of her grandparents' house. She didn't tell her squad that. Tonight, they only needed to hear about death. The water was warm in the late summer, and she used to sink to the bottom and grab onto a rock so she wouldn't float back to the surface. If she pinched her nose, she could turn over and look as sunlight reflected against the water. She didn't have the words or desire to describe the feeling of being submerged, tucked away from the world outside. Nor did she understand the feelings she was trying to cope with, the residue of the adult concerns that surrounded her at home.

Her grandmother didn't like her hiding under the water, but her grandfather indulged, as he did with most things regarding his granddaughter. They were both important people, one the former captain of the original convoy that took settlers to the new home. The other was ambassador for an entire planet, and then for an entire alien race.

All the young Jiao knew was that it was quiet and empty and safe down there. Summers on Pounamu meant lots of opportunities to disappear under the water, or in the woods behind the house, and even off shore with grandfather on his relic of a yacht. Leaving everything behind was easy on a boat—just cast off and the world went away. When she was older her grandfather let her take it out by herself. Then she really was alone. She loved that feeling. It was not something she felt very much in the years that followed.

And none of that mattered anymore.

Lao Lao Fran looked at her, face placid but eyes full of concern. That time when she was sick, bending over Jiao's fevered body and placing a cool cloth on her brow—that was a different kind of concern than the one expressed when grandfather overindulged. It was that look that made the young Jiao aware that her illness was serious. She didn't tell her squad anything about her grandparents. They knew who they were, and they knew better than to talk about them, at least when she was within earshot. She wasn't a Jensen anymore, or anything that name might bring with it. She was just Sarge. She was the one that would make sure they made it out alive. Or at least try, even if she pretended not to.

The jungle wheezed, as if a bunch of phlegmatic old men crouched in the bushes around them. In reality it was the movement of a creature that fit somewhere between an insect and a reptile, folding and unfolding the segments of its abdomen, to attract a mate, repulse anything wanting to eat it, or just to annoy the humans nearby. Jiao didn't care why it did it. The sound meant there was nobody else in that particular place and she could carry on talking without suddenly finding her head separated from her body.

"Yeah," Jiao said. "I was dying. That's what was happening."

"You're a morbid bitch," Unk said.

His age let him get away with more than others. He wasn't ten years older than those around him, but it was enough to make him the old man of the group. Uncle. Simply surviving that long earned him some privileges the newbies wouldn't dare exercise. Like calling Sarge a bitch. From him, she seemed to take it as compliment.

"Who doesn't think about death?" Jiao answered, gesturing to the dark bush around them. "I mean, seriously."

"No. You're dark," Unk added.

He looked across the circle and grinned at the young woman. The others let their eyes shift between the two. Les was actually corporal, second in command, but even he deferred to Unk, who was part of the squad before any of the others joined. He and Jiao were all that was left of the original members.

"No, I'm not," Jiao said. "I'm just not afraid to talk about it. I'm not afraid to face it."

"Are you saying I am?" Unk asked.

"Not you," she replied, letting her pause be clear for the others to understand who she was talking about. All of them.

"I'm calling macho shit," Nick said.

"What?" Jiao growled.

"Tough talk, that's all it is." He gazed at the patch of dark soil between his feet. He had only seen action once, a confused, brief skirmish the day before and he was still trying to hide his fear behind bravado.

"Face it, man," Jiao said. "We're not getting out of this alive, even if we survive the Beakers on this island. There will be another island. The sooner you stop thinking you'll live, the easier you'll sleep." She heard herself laying it on thick, but who knows, it might help keep them alive knowing they were already dead.

"Beakers are kicking our asses," Runt muttered. "On every fucking island."

"Easy, little guy," Unk said. "Tide will turn."

"Already fucking dead," Runt whispered.

"No way," Popper said from across the small circle. "I'm making it out."

"What did you say?" Jiao asked.

"I mean, 'No way, Sarge," Popper replied, adding a limp handed salute. He came with the name, and probably had it even before the Beakers rained down from their ships and crashed the party. He was just too familiar with the pills or powder he always seemed to be taking and dispensing.

"That's better," she said. "I'm not obsessing about death, I'm just talking about the moment. That moment when you know death is there—and only that moment. We're all gonna die, and let's face it, it will be sooner than we want. But in that moment, not to cry or whine or regret or beg for more life, but to say, 'thanks'. That's the mind frame you need right now."

"Thanks for *what*?" Nick asked.

Jiao bit her lip to stop it from rising. These new kids weren't good at knowing when to talk and when to just shut up and listen. Especially this one. At least not yet. If he made it through the next day, she might have to kick some learning into his ignorant ass.

"For the moment, man. Just the moment," she said.

"*Thanks*? For this shit?"

"Not this shit. Well, sure, some of it," she said. "Like this fine little moment we're having here."

"Sarge has been K-ping too much," Les said. "Popper's a bad influence."

"Best kind of influence," Popper said. "And pass it around. That stuff's hard to get."

The smaller man to his right handed him a vial filled with powder and a small slender spoon. He filled the bowl of the spoon, raised it to his nose and sniffed. Then he handed the vial around the circle as the chemical both sharpened his senses and deadened any sense of self. Ketamine, a dissociative anesthetic sanctioned and even encouraged by Command. Popper was the closest thing to a medic the squad had.

"Enough of your shit," Sanskrit said to the young men beside him. "Sarge speaks it. Let the moment come and watch it with wonder. Be able to say, 'this is my death moment' and step without fear into the next incarnation."

"Fuck your Buddhist shit," Unk said through a smile nobody could see. "You're both morbid fucks." Unk took the vial and filled the spoon with as much powder as possible. The others heard a sharp snort as he inhaled.

The forest darkened as the canopy hid the last rays of the setting sun. Sunset came quickly in the tropics, and soon an even thicker darkness wrapped around them. The wheezing beyond them continued, joined by a clicking of the wings of a nocturnal bird like creature. They were hard to see, but following the sound always led to a glimmer indicating its forward-facing eye. The sounds were reassuring to Jiao. Unk also relaxed, and the others recognized the creatures in the dark were the best sentinels they had. But not the small one—he twitched with anxiety, even with a nose full K. Jiao hoped he would relax into his situation before his nerves got him or somebody else killed.

"What time is it?" Runt asked.

"Who cares," Nick said. "Beakers are nowhere near."

"Always assume the Beakers are near," Jiao said.

"Thought you didn't care about dying."

"No man," she said. "I care. I'm just not going to whine about it."

"Sarge ain't allowed to whine," Les said. "Comes with the rank."

"Damn straight," Jiao agreed. "It's in the regs."

"Talking about it is just whining and crying," Nick said.

"No," Jiao said. "And you need to pack that attitude. Whining and crying is whining and crying. We've all seen that. Now shut the fuck up and realize the difference."

The others shifted uneasily, or stared at the ground, or scratched aimlessly in the dirt with a twig or finger. Not because of her rebuke, but because they all heard the cries, deep in the jungle. Beakers had pinned down a recon squad and picked them off slowly. Except for the last, who they cut apart, piece by piece, trying to snare another squad, suckering them forward in an attempt to save a comrade. That was the day before, or the day before that. Time had little meaning in retreat, and it was pointless to keep track.

They heard sounders not far away, the crack of tree limbs as the compressed sound waves tore through the vegetation. They were totally ineffective weapons in this kind of environment. The dense vegetation interrupted and dispersed their charge. Then they heard plasma blasts. And screaming. Les was already on his feet and moving forward before Sarge swung the butt of her plasma rifle and knocked his feet out from under him. He lay grasping his bruised shin, and the others lay still and very quiet as she ordered them with her eyes to stand down and stay still while the screaming and crying continued for what felt like hours.

They still heard it, even though it had died out with the poor son of a bitch's last breath. It took a long time for him to die, and Jiao and her squad lay still in the underbrush listening to every second of it. When it finally ceased, they stayed where they were, not moving a muscle and breathing as lightly as possible. They waited until long after the last footsteps receded before creeping into the kill zone and examining what was left. Nobody spoke as Sarge tore off dog tags and pocketed them. They silently watched as she moved from one mutilated corpse to the other.

"Fucking Beakers," Nick said, breaking the silence.

"Originals died here too," Jiao said.

"They're all fucking Beakers," Nick added. "Good riddance."

Jiao stepped over a corpse and stood in front of Nick, breathed in slowly and exhaled before slapping the man across the face. The others turned at the sound, even Runt, who continued wiping vomit from his chin.

"They're fighting for us," Jiao said. "They're dying for us. I will not have them disrespected in my squad. That screaming you heard? That wasn't an Original. Originals don't whine when they die, they just fucking do it. And they do it for us."

Nick let his eyes leave Jiao's. She was brought up to respect the race of aliens the humans found on the planet, the almost reverent view her grandfather held of the ancient species. She also fought beside them. Nick glanced at the large body under a nearby tree, its torso torn open by a plasma blast, before shifting his gaze to a bloody mass staked to the ground, all that remained of the sounds of the previous night. He didn't feel any different about Beakers or Originals, but he now knew enough not to say it around the sergeant. He tasted blood in his mouth and returned his gaze to the woman in front of him.

"How did they find them?" Popper asked. He put a small vial to his nose and sniffed. He didn't want to feel anything, especially there.

"I don't know," Jiao answered without turning, eyes still fixed on Nick's. It didn't take long to size up her new replacements. This one might be functional, but he would need some breaking.

"Maybe they got lucky. Had to happen sometime," she added.

"Oh, fuck me," Runt said.

"Stow it," Jiao ordered. "Grab whatever's useful and form up. Stalking formation."

"We're going after them?" Les asked.

"That's our job," Jiao said.

"Roger that," he answered, but she could hear the replacement corporal's reluctance. Yet another trooper needing some fine tuning. Not a good sign when non-comms come like that.

"How many do you reckon?" he asked.

"Eight, maybe more."

"I'd say twelve," Unk said.

"Then there's twelve," Jiao nodded. "Moving northwest because that is where we were. Only we're not there now, we're behind them. Form up. It's time to go hunting."

She watched as the squad walked gingerly through the kill zone, most of them seeing death for the first time. They had to harden up or they wouldn't last the week. Then she'd have even more replacements to break in. She glanced at Unk, who answered her silent question with an almost imperceptible move of his head.

"You fuckers ever whine or cry, I will shut you up for good, you can be certain of that," Jiao said. She knew what they were thinking about because she was thinking it too. Even in the dark she saw the fear on their faces as they remembered the ambush. "You've already been given too much. You have no reason to whine or cry. If I cry, I will shut myself up. We get fucked, we take it. No matter how hard, you fucking take it, and all those Beakers ever see is a fucking grin of gratitude on your faces as they cut you up or whatever the fuck they want to do. Do you hear me?"

"Yeah."

"Good," Jiao said. "You'd better.'

"You're a morbid bitch," Unk said. "But it's why we love you."

Jiao ignored him. "Pair up and take turns resting. We're hunting tomorrow, so get prepped. Get to your posts and keep your fucking eyes and ears open. Sort your shit, because you're going to need it. Payback when we find these Beakers."

"Fuck me," Runt said. "I mean, fuck yeah." Laughter crept around the circle, dying out with a glare form their sergeant.

"Okay," Jiao said. "Shut up now and get away from me. Les, spread them out."

"On it, Sarge," Les answered.

As the squad took positions in the nearby underbrush Unk stood close and spoke softly. "Nice pep talk."

"They needed to hear it." She shook her head. "Fucking command sends us these."

"They're all we got. Maybe they're all they had."

Unk recognized the sharp outbreath as close to a laugh Jiao ever had.

"Do *you* think they saw them?" she asked.

"No," Unk said. "The foliage was too ... it was all too fucked up. It looked like blind shooting."

"Agreed. Go on."

"I'd say they lured them, or waited until they reached that place, then opened up on the thermal signature," Unk added.

"What else?" Jiao asked.

"They shouldn't be able to see us yet," he said. "It took us months to adjust and see any wildlife when we arrived."

"Maybe the Beakers adjust quicker."

It was improbable, but the thought was still there, especially after seeing the carnage they can inflict in a fire-fight. But anybody returning to the planet had to adjust to the pheromones emitted by the vegetation, or to begin emitting them themselves.

"Or maybe they got help. Maybe they got GLR," Unk said. "They say it helps to see quicker."

"They say it does a lot of things," Jiao said.

"It does do a lot of things."

"No," Jiao said. "They haven't adjusted, and they're not dropping GLR." She looked over her shoulder at her squad taking positions for the night. "We're sticking to the plan."

She waited for any argument Unk might offer, share any niggles or doubts, but he remained silent.

"Send Les, will you? I'll run him through it one more time."

"On it," he said, already walking away.

Dawn came fast in the tropics. Jiao woke her squad before it came, and as light began to filter through the bush they silently made their way through the undergrowth. Runt moved next to her, the whites of wide eyes showing through the heat dampening camouflage paint that covered his face and any exposed skin. Command still didn't know if worked. It was her job to find out. One of her jobs. Assess effectiveness of heat dampening camouflage. Assess Beaker visual ability. Assess Beaker tactics and capabilities in jungle warfare, especially development of tactics. Assess any unfamiliar Beaker weapon technology, and if possible, return with artefact(s). Assess Beaker numbers, location of strongholds, etc. etc. It was a long wish list. The last orders she looked forward to fulfilling: eliminate Beaker presence once reconnaissance complete. Oh yeah, and return with information-slash-evidence.

She caught Les' eye, made a fist and pumped it up and down twice. "Pick it up." He increased the pace. Their path made a sweeping curve through the jungle. Their destination was only five klicks away, but the route made it almost twice that. There was a good reason for that course—if they went straight, they would run right into the Beaker patrol. By circling they came out in front and right in the invaders path. Jiao wasn't a patient person. Her grandfather had a saying, something about killing two birds with one stone. He told her 'birds' were feathered and flying creatures on mother earth, and showed her pictures when she still looked perplexed. But she got the idea. She would try twelve Beakers and Command's shopping list with one trick. She thought it was a good one. It would either work, or kill them all. Either way, the job would be over.

Les reached the kill zone first and dispersed the squad as instructed. Nick wiped sweat from his brow and began climbing a tree. Sanskrit picked a tree five meters away and climbed it. Runt buried himself in underbrush and Popper selected a tree further along. Jiao carried his drugs. She didn't want any troopers numb. She wanted them keyed up, even scared, waiting for their last moment.

Unk laughed quietly as those in the trees hung upside down. He didn't know if Jiao made them do it just to keep them angry. She said it was to confuse the Beakers, that if they could actually see them it might confuse their eyes. It worked with humans—we often look right past what we don't expect to see. Like men upside down in trees. But Beakers weren't human, and Sarge was probably full of shit. Unk climbed a tree, bent his knees around a limb and the jungle turned upside down. He watched Jiao bury herself in underbrush, catching a glimpse of the raised lip of her mirthless smile before she disappeared. He had to admit, it was an impressive net. If the Beakers walked into it.

He didn't have to wait long. A Beaker on point appeared without a sound and strode slowly beneath Unk. It stepped centimeters from where Runt lay and stopped. It scanned the area, the barrel of his weapon following his gaze. Unk realized he was holding his breath and inhaled carefully, quietly, hoping the twitchy kid below was holding still. From the height of the tree limb, the Beaker didn't seem so tall. But Runt must be gazing up at a giant. On the ground, Beakers stood a head taller than a tall human, and were wider as well, particularly at the shoulders. All muscle. The Beaker looked up and scanned the trees. Unk stared into his deep-set black eyes, the creature's long sharp noise pointing right at him. Unk now deliberately held his breath, finger on the trigger, waiting for the Beaker to act.

Instead, it continued to scan the trees. It made a low sound, somewhere between a croak and moan, and another Beaker wearing a device over its eyes entered, scanning the area. It paused when it looked at Jiao's hiding place, but continued on after a second that felt like an hour. The two moved forward and more followed. He counted twelve by the time the Beaker on point reached the edge of their trap. Before he stepped out of it, he fell forward with a bloody hole punched through his back. Like the Beaker, Unk never heard the blast from Jiao's rifle, but it was the cue for what came next. Instinct kicked in. Unk fired from above, his first shot taking a Beaker's head off, the second missing the Beaker with the device. The third and fourth and fifth shots hit their target. The device seemed to fall from its grasp in slow motion and Unk made a mental note where it landed as he sought another target. Other Beakers fell as fire rained down on them, or up from the bushes. Beakers that were fast enough fired blindly around them, until they also lay bloody on the jungle floor.

Silence returned as quick as it left. The air reeked of burning vegetation and cooked flesh. Three sharp whistles sounded and Jiao climbed out of her hide. Those in trees dropped down and joined her. She pointed at Les, indicated the trail behind and he disappeared without a sound. He came back moments later.

"Clear," he reported.

"Good," Jiao answered. "Where's Runt?"

"He's over here," Nick said, a slight waver in his voice.

"Send him."

"He can't come," Nick said.

Jiao bit back the urge to swear at the man and instead walked over to him. Runt lay ten meters away. His upper torso was still intact. The plasma burst that hit him removed everything below his chest. She bent down and tore off his dog tags.

"Fucking Beakers," Nick said.

"Fucking unlucky," Jiao said. She walked past him and back into the kill zone.

Unk was already holding the goggle like device seen from the tree, trying to get it to function.

Jiao patted his shoulder as she passed. "Bag it and carry on. See what else you can find."

"Les," she said to the corporal, "finish getting what we came for so we can leave."

She knelt beside a dead Beaker. She placed the back of her hand against the flesh of its face and felt the ebbing warmth. Beakers were warm blooded, mammalian, bipedal—not too dissimilar to humans. Except for their size and strength, and that nose that earned them their name. She pulled a large knife from her belt and made an incision around the Beaker's eye sockets. With thumb and forefinger she plucked the creature's eye out. The optic nerve and connective tissue stretched as she pulled. She cut it with her knife and placed the severed organ in a sterile specimen bag.

"We desecrating corpses now?" Nick asked. "I like it."

"It's hard to study optic ability without something to study, private," she said.

"Didn't seem like they could see us," he answered.

"Didn't seem. That means we still don't know. Have you got what you're after?"

He shook a rucksack in one hand. "Yes, sir," he answered.

She stood, resisting the urge to hit him. Or worse. She would deal with his attitude soon, just not here and now. "Then shoulder that and get ready to move," she said.

She didn't wait for an answer before she went to another dead Beaker. This one was mostly intact, at least beneath its neck. She removed a small case and withdrew a vial and small pair of scissors. Spreading the fingers of the creature's hand, she snipped out a triangle of skin. Taking tweezers from the case, she lifted the small flap of skin and placed it in the vial. The lab techs were adamant she obtained at least three samples, so she took four, spreading the thumb and forefinger and snipping a large piece. She cut it into smaller pieces so it could fit into the last vial.

Command also requested a blood sample. There was enough of that around. But they wanted it fresh from a vein. They recommended the carotid, or at least the Beaker equivalent. She glanced at the gaping hole where anything taking blood to the brain was just as absent as any brain. She ran her hand up the Beaker's thick arm and located a vein, inserted the syringe the techs provided and pulled back the plunger. To her surprise, the barrel filled with a small amount. It would have to do. She withdrew and capped the syringe and placed it in its case.

"We ready, Les?" she called.

"We're ready," he replied.

"Then let's head out. Stay sharp. And move fast," she said. "There'll be follow up soon. Lead the way, corporal."

Les set out a brisk run, followed by the rest of the squad. Jiao retreated up the incoming path and strung a trip wire between two trees, attaching a charge that was more sound than fury. Returning to the site of the ambush, she took a last look at the scene, including the crumpled remains of Runt.

"You just got there before us, kid," she said before following the others. "Rest easy. You earned it."

NUMBER FIFTY-TWO

Number Fifty-Two woke, folded back her blanket and rose. She stood naked in the large room and stepped to the end of her bed. There, as on every morning, she found a folded gown and put it on. The loosely fitting garment was comfortable, but she didn't know the word for comfort. Number Fifty-Two didn't know words. She understood, and made, a few simple signs. She saw Number Twelve standing nearby, risen and clothed. She wiped her hand across her mouth.

Good morning. Hello.

Number Twelve wiped his hand across his mouth. They both wore smiles. Another form of communication. She followed him to the ablution room, went to her cabinet and withdrew her toothbrush. She cleaned her teeth. Then she removed her gown, hung it on a hook, and entered the shower. She pressed a button in the wall and warm water flowed over her body. She accessed a dispenser and filled a palm with liquid soap. She rubbed it over her body. It was important to keep clean.

When she finished washing, she stood under a blow dryer. Number Twelve stood beside her, and beside him stood numbers Eighteen and Twenty-Two. The hot hair dried their bodies and then shut off. Each went to a moisture dispenser and applied lubricant to their skin. When finished, they entered the nutrient room. Number Fifty-Two took her tray and removed the cover. She smiled. She liked the nutrient tray after washing. She liked the sensation the salted egg caused on her tongue, though she didn't know the words for sensation or egg or tongue.

Number Fifty-Two finished her meal, brought her hand to her chin and removed it. Thank you, she told the tray. She smiled and looked at those around her. Fifty-Two typically wore a smile. She liked being around the others. She felt comfort, companionship, even love. Number Fifty-Two did not know any of those words. But she felt them.

After breakfast, Fifty-Two and the others made their way to Supplements, a window where they were given a small cup containing pills and another containing water. Fifty-Two placed the pills in her mouth and swallowed them with the water. She then made her way to another room filled with exercise equipment. Fifty-Two didn't know the word for exercise. Except for one day each month, it was a daily routine she followed, part of keeping her body healthy. The sign for exercise was both hands balled into fists and rotating rapidly. Fifty-Two mounted a running treadmill, pressed the start button, and followed a program designed specifically for her physical needs. After the treadmill she went to each prescribed machine, working upper and lower body. After the session, she returned to the shower room and cleansed. It was important to keep clean.

A fresh gown was waiting for her after she had dried her body. Fifty-Two put it on and returned to the dormitory. She sat on the edge of her bed and took rest. She watched as others came in from breakfast or exercise and took rest on their beds. She did not understand why some did not follow her routine, why each seemed to have a routine slightly different from hers. But she did not know words or concepts such as routine, or different, or hers. Fifty-Two smiled as she watched the others return to sit on their beds. It was quiet time. Fifty-Two felt a warmth deep inside, emanating from her belly and spreading throughout her whole being. She did not know the word for contentment. But she was content.

Fifty-Two looked across the room at Thirty-Five and felt discomfort. Thirty-Five had an expression that resembled a grimace. Fifty-Two did not know the word 'frown', but recognized that Thirty-Five was not content. She rose from her bed and walked to that of Thirty-Five. She looked at Thirty-Five and placed a hand over her chest, looking down as she did.

Are you okay? You look unwell. I am concerned.

Thirty-Five quickly raised her hand to her chin and lowered it. Thank you.

Fifty-Two was at a loss for words, because she knew none. Thirty-Five lifted her gown and displayed a large scar on her abdomen. The bright red of the wound looked angry. Black threads protruded from her skin, a suture holding the woman's flesh together. Fifty-Two ran her hand slowly in a downward motion across her mouth. I am sad for you. Thirty-Five did not respond, only gazed at the wound on her side. As Fifty-Two did not have words, she acted. She sat beside Thirty-Five on Thirty-Five's bed. It was the first time she sat on another's bed. And for the first time, she touched another. She put her arm around Thirty-Five and pulled her close. Then she put her other arm around Thirty-Five.

Nobody taught Fifty-Two how to hug, but that is what she did. She felt the body of Thirty-Five shiver, as if she were in cold water. Fifty-Two felt her shoulder grow moist as water left Thirty-Five's body through her eyes. Fifty-Two was familiar with water leaving through eyes. Late at night, alone in her bed and for reasons she did not understand nor have words to explain, water left her eyes and moistened her pillow. So, she did not mind the other woman's water wetting her gown. She continued to hold Thirty-Five.

When Thirty-Five stilled she pulled back and wiped her face. She looked at Fifty-Two, perplexed and also pleased. She touched her chin and lowered her hand. Thank you. Fifty-Two touched her hand in response, leaving hers on the others. Fifty-Two felt the urge to gently squeeze Thirty-Five's hand, so she did. They sat together, holding hands, until a bell chimed. It was time for afternoon nourishment. They rose together and made their way to the Nutrient room situated beside their sleeping area.

Fifty-Two liked the middle feed. It was typically warm and salty. Fifty-Two did not know about salt but she took pleasure from the way the taste squeezed her tongue and left it dry. Some meals made her whole face warm, and some tastes caused the heat to rush down her torso and even into her crotch. She did not understand that tingling. But she liked it. It was the same sensation she got when watching Twelve in the ablution room, after morning exercise and he was washing his body under jets of warm water. Fifty-Two smiled as she finished her meal.

During the afternoon Fifty-Two joined others on stretching exercises, followed by visual stimulation where she followed dancing lights without moving her head, and then slow walking on the treadmills. One treadmill was unoccupied and she searched for Nine, who usually walked upon it. During evening nourishment she scanned the nutrient room for Nine, but could not see her. When all filed to their beds, Fifty-Two walked close to Nine's, but it was empty and Nine was not to be seen. Fifty-Two made her way to her own bed, removed her gown and dropped it on the floor. In the morning it would be cleaned and folded neatly at the foot of her bed.

Fifty-Two crawled under her covers and lay still, but could not sleep. The image of Thirty-Five invaded her mind, the pained look on the other woman's face that Fifty-Two could not understand. Then Fifty-Two thought of the empty bed that belonged to Nine. She did not think in words as she did not have any, but the images and feelings were strong enough. Fifty-Two felt her body shake and her pillow grew moist as water inexplicably escaped from her eyes. She sniffed and wiped her nose on her pillow.

And then, like holding Thirty-Five's hand, she acted impulsively, not understanding why, simply responding to a physical and emotional need she could not articulate. Fifty-Two rose from her small bed and quietly stepped past others until she reached the bed where Twelve slept. Without word or sign, she lifted the cover and got in next to him. She lay on her side and wriggled back as close as possible. He nestled around her, holding her in an embrace. It was an instinctual response that he could not understand or articulate, but he liked her warmth and closeness. Fifty-Two felt a hardness press against her bottom. It slowly subsided as Twelve's breathing became slower as he fell asleep. Fifty-Two lay in his arms for several hours feeling comforted. She did not know the word, only the need. Finally, as the night continued in endless darkness, she gently lifted Twelve's arm and slid out of his bed. She crept back to her own and was soon asleep.

Number Fifty-Two woke, folded back her blanket and rose. She stood naked in the large room and stepped to the end of her bed. A gown lay folded neatly. She surveyed the room before putting it on.

Others were rising and donning their garment. Each wore the same type of gown. It was white, but Fifty-Two didn't know names for colors. Once dressed, all those in the room looked the same. There were no mirrors in the complex, and Fifty-Two did not know that the similarity did not stop at their gowns. Every female had the same hair, the same features and the same face. In her small world, there were many females but only one face, just as there were many males, and yet only one.

Fifty-Two knew others by differences, some obvious, and others not. Three-Two-Four wore a bandage on her face that covered where she once had an eye. Thirty-Five had a large scar on her abdomen. Two-Oh-Seven always wore a bandage on the inside of her arm where blood was harvested daily. The reason for the bandage was not known to Fifty-Two. She merely noticed its presence. Sixty-Four, Twenty-Eight, Four-Three-Nine, and many other females had great swellings in their bellies. When they were close to bursting their tight skin moved as if something was inside wishing to be out. Each female disappeared into the clinic before that ever happened, returning to the dormitory with empty, sagging skin.

Others wore different bandages or scars. And still others seemed to be invisibly scarred, despite any outward marks. Eighteen was spiteful and to be avoided if at all possible. Again, Fifty-Two could not articulate that judgement, she simply kept a distance from the woman. Like she did with the male, One-Eight-One. Every female kept away from him, especially after the lights went out. Twelve had a smell the other males did not possess. When it filled Fifty-Two's nostrils she felt a warmth inside, a quiet comfort that did not exist elsewhere in her world. To Fifty-Two, Twelve was as different from the other males in the room as black is to white. She knew this without words such as 'black' or 'white'.

Fifty-Two continued to watch the others as they dressed and made their ways to the ablution room, nutrition, exercise or clinic, depending on their individualized schedule. Her entire world was actually one large room, divided by internal walls and doors. Her eyes rose to the ceiling high above. Her gaze moved from left to right as they scanned the vast ceiling that framed her life. She examined the walls separating the vast space into smaller designated zones. She watched as her sisters and brothers disappeared through doorways.

A movement nearby distracted her study and she turned to see an Attendant. His face was different from the males she lived with. Each Attendant wore the same garments, loose fitting trousers and smock of a color that Fifty-Two did not know the word for. The color of the floor. But aside from their clothing, they all looked disturbingly different—their shape, size, face, hair. Fifty-Two did not have a word for the discomfort she felt in their presence. She merely felt. And as the Attendants played such a vital role in her existence, she simply carried the feeling, as no other option existed.

The Attendant made a simple sign. He opened both hands. Fifty-Two tilted her head, trying to comprehend. He similarly tilted his head, moving one hand an inch towards her, and she understood.

Are you alright, Fifty-Two?

She made a small smile and tilted her head forward briefly. I am fine.

The Attendant moved his hand forward another inch, and then pointed it towards the gown that lay folded at the foot of her bed. Fifty-Two looked at herself and noticed her nakedness, or more accurately, that she was not wearing her gown. After she slipped it on, the Attendant made another sign. He balled his hands into fists and rotated them rapidly. That sign had many meanings, each relating to circumstances.

In this case it meant: Are you ready? Please hurry.

Fifty-Two glanced at the ablution room and the Attendant signed again. He balled his hands into fists and rotated them rapidly. His mouth made a downward arch. Hurry, you are already late. I am displeased with this delay.

Fifty-Two walked to the ablution room, voided her bladder, washed her body, dried, and returned. The Attendant gestured to another door and began walking towards it. Fifty-Two followed. She knew the door and the routine that awaited inside the other room. She went to the clinic in the middle of each of her cycles, every month. She entered the room and removed her gown, hanging it on a hook beside the door. She sat in the reclining chair indicated by the female Attendant in the clinic. Fifty-Two lifted each leg and docilely allowed the Attendant to bend her knees and strap each foot in the stirrups mounted on the chair. She felt warm and soapy water on her groin, and then the scraping of a razor over the stubble remaining from the previous month's procedure. Once finished, the Attendant dried the area between Fifty-Two's legs.

Another Attendant, male, wheeled a device over to where Fifty-Two sat. He removed a syringe and Fifty-Two closed her eyes as the needle pricked her skin. She felt numbness spread throughout her body. She opened her eyes as gel was rubbed over her lower abdomen and watched as a handheld device pressed into her flesh. The Attendant studied a screen, dark with bright marks. She closed her eyes again as fingers probed her intimately and a speculum was inserted into her vagina. Fifty-Two always kept her eyes closed during this part of the procedure. The numbness dulled the experience, but the fine needle passing through her vaginal wall and into each follicle of her ovary caused discomfort and fear. As with so many areas of her life, she had no comprehension of what was actually happening.

Fifty-Two's eyes remained closed as the Attendant withdrew the needle and studied its contents. Only when the speculum was removed and her feet released did she open her eyes again. The male Attendant that led her to the clinic assisted her back to bed. He handed her a small paper cup with a blue pill inside, and another cup with water. She placed the pill in her mouth and swallowed it as she drank. Then she got into her bed and closed her eyes, waiting for a sleep that would carry her into the next morning.

LOST IN THE VOID

S ean followed the noise. A cry that escaped in gasps. He pulled his way along the dimly lit corridor and the sounds grew louder. Her cabin door was open so he floated in. Janis turned her puffy face in his direction, droplets of tears drifting away from her red eyes.

"I can't move my legs," she said. "I can't feel anything." Her body hung in the center of the room, upper torso animated, arm reaching out to him. Below the waist, her limbs trailed like loose fabric.

"I'm here, Janis." Sean pushed off the door frame lightly, took Janis's hand as he slowly passed and stopped both of them above her unkempt bed at the far wall. He wiped moisture from her eyes and ran his fingers gently down her swollen cheek.

"I'm here now," he repeated. He didn't say everything was going to be alright, because it wasn't. "Tell me what happened."

She grabbed his arm and upset their balance. The pair rotated slowly. "I turned to grab a handhold and felt a click and then I couldn't feel anything. My legs won't work, Sean. I can't move them!"

"It'll be okay," he said, despite not wanting to. He held her face in his hand and made eye contact until he could feel her grip relax. "I'll have a look. I'm going to need to check you, alright? Look at your legs?"

"Yes, yes," she said. "Anything."

"You said you weren't going to lie anymore," the boy said.

"It helps sometimes," Sean told him.

"Yes, of course. Anything, Sean," Janis said.

"Where did you feel the click?" Sean asked.

"Low." Janis let go of Sean's arm and tried to move her hand to her lower back. He stopped her and turned her body away so that her back faced him. He ran a hand over her shoulders, found her vertebra and followed them down. She confirmed sensation until he reached the lumbar region. At L 4 or maybe L 3 the bones shifted to the left.

"I'm just going to look at your back now, okay?" he asked.

"Of course. What do you see? What is it?"

"I don't know yet, Janis." Sean moved the fabric of her shirt up to reveal the smooth white skin of her lower back. Her trousers rose too high for him to see what he needed to see.

"You're lying again," the boy said. "You do know what it is."

Sean turned his head to the boy. The boy stood on the deck looking up at the two adults floating weightlessly above. Sean mouthed the words, go away, at the boy, but the boy didn't. Instead, he scratched his shaved head and replaced both hands on his hips.

"Your pants are in the way," Sean said to Janis. "I'll have to pull them down to look."

"Anything, Sean."

He pulled the elastic waist wide and slid her pants below her boney hips and over her emaciated bottom. The pants had absorbed all the fluid that escaped when she injured herself and her bladder voided itself, but several drops of urine still drifted away.

"These need to be cleaned, so I'll just take them all the way off and get you something fresh," he told her.

Janis cried quietly as he took them off, bunched them up and stuffed them into a plastic bag he had attached to his waist. For soiled garments, dirty bandages, other human waste and detritus. He learned that such a bag was useful to have. He pulled out a disposable moist towel and cleaned between her legs as he examined the damage. Purple bruising covered her lower back and spread down each butt cheek. Sean touched the bones where they misaligned and felt a slight give as the bone crumbled under his finger. How long since she used the muscles that supported her weight? For how long have her bones been degrading? How many RADs were they all exposed to? The boy was right, he did know what happened. Janis turned to grab the handhold and the twist fractured the weakened bones and severed her spinal cord.

"She's going to die," the boy said.

"We all are," Sean told him.

"We are all what?" Janis asked.

"We're all going to make it." He was a liar and didn't need the boy to nag him about it. Lying was probably the most useful thing he carried in the first aide bag strapped to his shoulders. "Can you keep hold there and I'll fetch you some fresh pants. What drawer?"

"Third."

"Great," Sean said. "And then I'll give you something to reduce inflammation. You have a nasty bruise down there. It happens. Probably pinched a nerve. I'm sure sensation will return, you just have to be patient. I know it's scary as hell, but it'll come right, okay?"

"Okay," she said, voice tinged with a remnant of hope.

He returned with clean pants and pulled them up to her waist. Then he turned her around so that she faced him. He smiled softly, moved his head closer and held his forehead against hers. She cried softly. When he moved back, tear drops hovered between them.

"Stay with me for a while?" she asked.

"I'm making my rounds," Sean told her. "But I'll be back."

Sean left her, legs dangling useless above the floor. Come on kid, he thought, as he floated out of her door and into the corridor. The boy padded along beside him as Sean pushed off the wall and continued floating forward. They passed a closed door.

"Aren't you going to go into that room?" the boy asked. "You never go in."

"I already know what's in there," Sean said.

"Why don't you put her with the others?"

"She likes her privacy."

"You always say that."

"So why do you keep asking?"

Sean stopped at another door and looked at the boy. The kid wore a pair of dirty tennis shoes whose soft soles barely made a sound on the decking. He had on blue jeans and a lined checked jacket covering a stained white t-shirt. The boy indicated to the door and Sean opened it. With a slight flick of his wrist he drifted into the room and joined its sole occupant. She was motionless in the zero gravity, arms slightly away from her body. Her glazed eyes stared past him, through the walls of the ship and into another existence. Small droplets of blood escaped a nostril and joined others as they were slowly sucked into the air vent. One of the few systems still functioning.

Yesterday she complained of intense headaches, caused by fluid pooling in her skull and creating increased pressure against the backs of her eyes. No gravity to take it down. He gave her powerful painkillers from the kit he carried. Was it a Stroke? Thrombosis? Were they the same thing? Sean was well aware he was out of his depth. The ship's doctor and her assistant died in the initial incident. He had a little more than the rudimentary first-aide training all crew received, so appointed himself medic and started making rounds to the survivors. It gave he and the boy something to do. It wasn't a complete waste of time if it did that, right?

"Oh, Debbie," Sean said, taking one of her hands. "I hope that head feels better." He pushed off a wall and led her out of the room and down the corridor. They passed several empty rooms until reaching a closed door. It used to be a storage bay, and still was, in a way. He opened the door, kissed Debbie's cold cheek, and pushed her through. She drifted into the room, joining the twenty-three other silent occupants. He closed the door.

"I don't like that room," the boy said.

"Neither do I," Sean replied. "At least they're together."

"She would like to join them."

"Don't start," Sean snapped. He collected himself quickly. "Let's go to the bridge. You like it there, don't you?"

"I do," the boy said.

Sean pushed away from the storage room and floated down another corridor and the boy hurried to keep up, tennis shoes now slapping as he ran.

"Permission to enter the bridge, Captain?" Sean said at a large entrance.

"Don't call me that! I'm not the captain!" a voice growled back.

Yes, you are, Sean thought. The captain is dead, and you are now the ranking officer, regardless of how low that rank might have been before the shit rained down. Sean didn't remember John's rank prior to the event. Third mate? Junior engineer?

"Sorry. Mind if I come in, John?" Sean said.

"Of course, don't be stupid," John said.

He sat facing a dead control panel. Sean floated close to him, holding the panel to stop momentum. The captain who refused to admit he was captain wore a grim expression.

"It's fried," he said.

"Still," Sean added.

"Shut up," John said. "We're fucked, you know that don't you? The SPE fried everything, including most of the crew. The computer went berserk and ordered an acceleration—"

"Phantom command," Sean said, having heard most of this before.

"Fuck... fucking whatever... it sent us out of the shipping lane. Way out of the elliptical. And fucking fried everything."

"Captain's beacon would have gone off," Sean said.

When he realized all electrics, including emergency beacons, were fried by the solar particle event—a massive radiation storm—the captain boarded an escape boat, ejected from the crippled ship and manually activated a working locator beacon. He sacrificed his life, as the craft had limited oxygen and he was already exposed to fatal doses of radiation, but the beacon could alert any ship nearby of their distress. Only his corpse was now thousands of kilometers away from the ship he was trying to save. The captain's beacon, if it went off, would not have helped anybody on his ship. The radiation of the event condemned any surviving to a slow and painful death. Even if help arrived this very minute, it would be too late.

But basic life support on the stricken vessel kicked in. Dim lighting in all the corridors—a shadowland for the dying. Ventilation and water recycling. Plentiful food supplies. All allowed the dead to live another day.

"Can I play with the controls?" the boy asked.

"Why not, they don't work," Sean said.

"You still got that kid following you around?" John asked.

"Yeah. Can't seem to shake him." But Sean enjoyed the strange company.

"You're losing it, man," John said. "Your brain is fried. You realize there is no boy?"

"Of course. And you are no doubt correct about my brain. But I'm here for you. How are the eyes?"

"Everything is a blur, fading fast. And my arm does shit I don't tell it to."

"Hey, I know that one," Sean said. "That's ataxia. You lose control of coordination and muscle movement. It'll spread to other limbs. You're fucked. Sorry."

"Great bedside manner," John said. "Anything you got in that bag for the eyes? I'd really like to pretend like I was doing something. I mean, there's got to be something."

'Yeah, I think I do," Sean said. He looked at the boy, who looked back accusingly. Liar. "Let me use these cleansing drops, and a pill that'll cause some numbing, which is what the muscles need."

"Anything, man," John said. "Let's do it."

Sean placed the dropper against John's eye and closed his lids as he finished, ensuring the moisture didn't float away. Then he gave him a sedative. John took the pill. He would feel a warmth throughout his wrecked body, as well as a sense of general wellbeing. Everything was going to work out. The electronics would re-start. He would discover where they are, restart the engines and guide them back to the shipping lane where their beacon would be heard and ... They watched as John smiled and went somewhere much nicer.

"You're an asshole," the boy said. "That pill's way too strong."

"And you don't know what you're talking about," Sean snapped.

"Let him face the truth," the boy said. "Seems fair enough."

"Nothing's fair about this," Sean said. "He can't face it, that's the whole point. That's why we're here."

"Right. And what about you? Can you face anything? Are you going to deal with that?"

Sean looked from the boy to his own arm. He unwrapped the tape and gauze and stuffed the soiled bandages into his bag. The ulceration had not improved. From the angry red and black he saw that the infection had fought off all the antibiotics he threw against it and was visibly rotting. He applied cream from his kit and rebandaged the wound. He pulled a leg up and peeked under the bandages to glimpse more seeping and weeping flesh, and didn't bother changing the bandage.

"Well," the boy demanded. "Are you going to face it?"

"Fuck off!" Sean shouted.

The boy stood, scratched his head and placed his hands on his hips. He watched the man floating above and shrugged.

"Francis probably needs fluids," the boy said. "Her gut is shot. She's shitting out her intestinal lining as we speak."

"No, you're right," Sean said. He pushed off the control panel and drifted towards the exit. "And sorry I told you to fuck off. Let's go check her out."

Message from Afar

T he first message took three months to decipher. It was clear
from its very structure that it was different. It came at regular
intervals and repeated itself. Both were features of the messages leaving
earth. It meant the message was deliberate, sent with the intention
to be heard. Sometimes that was all that was wanted. "Hello. We are
here," was the gist of many sent from earth. But after three months of
efforts to extract the information in the repeating pattern, three words
were understood. Those three words contained in binary notation
continued to repeat themselves for the remainder of the year, and then
a little into the next. For thirteen months, a three-word message was
broadcast from somewhere in the constellation Aquarius.

It said: "Message to follow."

Humanity unwittingly reached out to the stars as soon as radio
technology was created. Faint waves emanated from the planet, dis-
persing into the solar system and beyond at the speed of light. But if
any trace of these signals were ever detected by an intelligent species

on a distant world, they wouldn't be treated to the voice of Orson Wells describing an alien invasion, or re-runs of popular sitcoms, or the first televised transmission, that of Adolf Hitler announcing the beginning of the Berlin Olympics. Any electromagnetic signal would be degraded and consumed by the background static of the galaxy, mere radio waves leaking from the planet like drops of water from a saturated sponge.

Messages must be deliberate. Early efforts were physical, sent when crossing stellar distances relied solely on the ability to accelerate a craft through the vacuum of space. The Pioneer probe carried a plaque, engraved with the image a man and a woman, as well as a map of the solar system. Voyager brought with it a disc, which contained images, greetings in over fifty languages, and even music, including Louis Armstrong singing about what a wonderful world from which the craft originated. At its current velocity, Voyager will deliver that message to the nearest solar system in eighty thousand years.

Messages must be focused. In the year 2013 a brief note was sent to a red dwarf star located in the Boötes constellation named Gliese 526. It was a simple hailing, directions to the planet, an outline of the periodic table, and a definition of the hydrogen atom in binary code. It also directed any listener capable of deciphering it to a frequency where more messages existed. It was known as the Lone Signal Project, despite being many more than a single message. On that other frequency, messages of one hundred and forty-four characters were sent by anybody wishing to do so. The first message was free, but additional shouts into space cost a small fee. The Lone Signal Project shut down shortly after transmission began due to lack of funding.

Gliese 526 is seventeen light years from Earth, so the communication would not reach any exo-planet there for over seventeen years, and the reply, if any, another seventeen years to return. It was a shot in the dark, that depended on ears to hear it (a species with the technological ability to detect the physical phenomenon of the message) and the intellectual sophistication to perceive the information (a species with the sentience to comprehend it). Those behind the Lone Signal Project didn't stick around to wait for a response, moving on to other projects or schemes once they quickly went bankrupt. Their dream of a chain of satellite dishes across the globe beaming messages into space remained unfulfilled. In 2030, thirty-four years after the earth reached out, no response from Gliese 526 was detected by scientists keeping up an active search for extra-terrestrial life.

Proponents of METI (Messaging Extra-Terrestrial Life), like those behind the Lone Signal Project, shouted into the skies. It was a controversial approach, but done because ... it could be done. In 1974, a message was transmitted from the Arecibo radio telescope in Puerto Rico towards the M13 globular cluster, located over twenty-four thousand lightyears away. Nobody was planning on sticking around for the required forty-eight thousand years to listen for a response. The message celebrated the reopening of the telescope, and was sent just because it could. With the technology of the day, the message continued to degrade as it traveled and would never reach its target. But it was a celebration. As technology improved, so too did the messaging.

Not all were happy with this. Some asked, quite reasonably, whether it was safe to shout into a dark room, not knowing what was inside it. Any species with the technological ability to both listen to an informal invitation and then show up was certainly more advanced than humanity at that time. It was a science fiction trope, but a legitimate worry. The earth had been invaded many times, watched by millions, albeit on the silver screen. With imagination so vivid, the lack of response was desired. Others tried to explain the cosmic silence differently. The Zoo Hypothesis maintained that the silence was deliberate avoidance. As if a large sign stood near the exhibit: "Do not feed the animals." Others held that extra-terrestrial life was more benevolent, trying to prevent any interplanetary contamination. Or, as the Laboratory Hypothesis held, earth *was* the experiment. Just like sticking a finger in a petri dish, contact might contaminate results. Or, again hoping for benevolence, *they* simply were waiting until humanity reached a certain level of development, technologically, or morally.

It was all fantasy. The galaxy was big, and the space between stars immense, measured not by distance, but time. The time it took light to travel from one point to another. But even that time was not the same. Light from Gliese 526 reaching the earth was seventeen years old by the time it reached the planet. What was actually seen was a glimpse into the past. Chances were very good that a civilization on a planet in the globular cluster known as M13 may not even exist in forty-eight thousand years, once any listeners responded. With humanity's propensity towards conflict, it was valid to worry if it would even last another fifty, or one hundred years, let alone thousands. The Fermi Paradox maintained that the time between civilizations was just too great for two civilizations to ever meet. Even if an alien civilization existed one hundred thousand, ten thousand, or even a mere thousand years in the past, that was enough to never meet.

But dedicated listeners maintained their vigil. Satellites searched the heavens, from the planet, and in orbit. Scientists listened to distant radio waves and perceived echoes made mere microseconds after the Big Bang. As the ability to listen grew, humanity heard more, from closer to home, and within our own galaxy. By the time the first deliberate message was received and deciphered, humanity even had the technology to render distance, and time, irrelevant.

The alien message that followed was the most complex ever received. It took fourteen hours to fully download, and almost an entire year to decode. Every university and observatory with the capacity to do so worked on the incredible quantity of data. Only when it was discovered by a graduate student at the Bern Observatory that what she was looking at was not actually a message, but a lesson in linguistics, did the collective efforts start to pay off. The earth had been sent a Rosetta Stone in zeros and ones. The phonemes, digraphs, verbal conjugations and rules of grammar of an alien language were unlocked. At the end of the lesson were the three words already learned: "Message to follow."

In the third year, they introduced themselves.

THE COMMUTE

K ath inhaled deeply. The cabin smelled of lemon wood polish mixed with bleach. She smiled and stroked the dark wood with her eyes, as if it were a cat that she happened to live in. Checking the power was off for the third time, she stepped through the galley and climbed the steps to the cockpit. Sliding the panels in place, she slid the lid closed, encasing her home in dark. The padlock clicked shut, making it safe. The harbor master was the only other person with a key, and it was his job to keep an eye on all the boats in the marina. Walking down the jetty, she checked for the fourth time that the lines were secured to their cleats and the fenders cushioning the yacht against its moorings were in place. She was procrastinating, delaying, lingering with her love. She studied the lines of the classic boat, its native timber glassed with fibreglass and white paint.

Her vibrating phone stopped her from climbing on deck and rechecking the sail cover. The locked off halyard. The forward hatch. The anchor. Instead, she picked up her case and hefted it to the carpark where a driverless cab waited.

"One bag," she told the vehicle, and the trunk popped open. She lifted the case into the open space, told the car to close its hatch. The passenger door was already open and she sat inside.

"Thank you for using City Driverless, where we're—"

She cut off the machine. "Airport. Domestic Terminal."

"Arriving at Domestic Terminal in estimated thirteen minutes. Would you like to listen to music during your drive?" the car asked.

"Silence, please." Kath wondered why she used courtesy with a computer programme. She shrugged as the vehicle silently moved away from the marina and merged into the flow of traffic.

Living in the marina had its advantages. All today required was a bit of wood polishing, a short flight to the city, then another taxi to the space port. She used to spend more time preparing for a tour on Luna, but it was habitual now. Three months on, three months off. It was a job. At the spaceport she recognized her transit ship. It was old but had good food and a comfortable cabin. Comfortable enough. Not a bad way to spend the four days to reach base, and her pay started as soon as she boarded.

"Be safe!" her friends told her at the usual pre-departure get together.

They didn't understand that the most dangerous thing she could do on the tour was overeat but that kind of response was lost on them. She thought it was funny, even if they didn't get it. She left them thinking she was an adventurer. On the sea, or off the planet.

Boredom was actually the biggest danger. They might understand that, but she didn't want them to think of her work that way or disabuse them of their impression of her life. Days and weeks and months confined to a small base, keeping accounts and monitoring communications in Earth's most remote outpost that contained more machines than humans. It required a special mental set, a slowdown.

Time could drag insufferably if you thought about it too much. How many days served, how long to go until the transport home. Until fresh air and sun and friends and family. Kath didn't mind. Time on the sea made you slow down. Take every day for itself, not think about arriving, but just getting there. And although Kath missed home, and thought privately that each contract was a waste of her life, on another level she liked it. She saw things most people never would. She experienced things most could never understand. She took comfort in the long night that lasted two weeks. Felt as if it were a warm quilt wrapped around her body, swaddling her soul. The sense of loss when the light returned for its two weeks … She only shared that with her colleagues. Her friends definitely wouldn't get it. So few would. She liked being part of an exclusive club.

Kath stuffed a few clothes and toiletries in her bag, grabbed a couple of novels she knew she would never read. Earlier in the day, and before the taxi came, she took her home out for a last sail in the bay. The wind was perfect, a steady blow from the northwest. As soon as she cleared the break, she hoisted the main, leaving the helm on auto as she climbed on deck and manually worked the lines. Modern boats were mostly or totally computer controlled. Touch a button and a sail raises, program a degree and the boat self tacks. Computer reads the course and wind direction and trims the sails in an efficiency no human could equal. Bah. Kath enjoyed keeping watch and having sore hands after a sail. She liked needing to clip on to a guide line and loved the risk of injury or even death behind her every action. It made her feel alive.

The work paid for mooring, maintenance, and the last two loan repayments on the money she borrowed to buy it. Two more tours and she would be a home owner, even if that home was a seventy-year-old thirty-eight-foot sloop rigged yacht. It was hers, and much better than bricks and mortar because it could go anywhere. And bricks and mortar were not available to her generation. Home ownership was beyond the reach of most her age. And she was making it happen.

Kath hated leaving her boat, especially for the three months of her contract. But soon she would have no reason to go. Paid off, freehold. Free. Hold. That was the goal, the prize, the pot at the end of the rainbow. She could pick up whatever work she could find, whatever she needed, wherever she wanted. Wait tables, pour coffee, pick fruit. Anything. And she could go wherever, whenever, she wanted. No life in limbo on a Lunar base, no time doing time, to pay for more time.

After the sail, she obsessively checked all lines and hatches, gazed sadly at the polished hull that would need to be scraped and cleaned again when she returned, and climbed out of the driverless when it reached the terminal. She collected her bag and checked it through to her final destination. The flight was uneventful as usual, and she was at the vessel before noon. She put her bag at the bottom of the steps—a crew member would bring it to her quarters—and climbed into the ship. Launch was still four hours away, but noon was the time requested by the flight coordinator. He had a lot to organise, ensuring all stores and passengers were stowed in their proper place. Kath climbed to the bridge and introduced herself.

"Hi, I'm Kathleen Cannon, the accounts and comms replacement," she said.

"Hi Kathleen," a man said. He wore three days of stubble and had what Kath referred privately to as a spaceman's physique. Soft hands, weak legs and a pot belly. She waited for more.

"Just letting you know I'm aboard," she said. "I can see you're pretty busy."

"That's an understatement." He offered his hand and a limp shake. He smiled. "I'm John, the first mate. I'll have Peta show you your cabin, and a quick tour of the ship. She's the purser, in charge of all cargo and passengers. She'll look after you."

"Thanks," Kath said.

"Peta to bridge," the first mate said into a microphone mounted on the console.

Moments later a lean woman appeared and offered Kath her hand. The purser was the opposite of the first mate. Tall, athletic build, dreadlocks tied back, smile full of white teeth. Tanned skin. Kath imagined the young woman on her yacht. She looked like she would be fun to sail with. Strong hands pulling lines, or lean body lying on the deck in the sun. It was a nice picture. She stored the image for the long weeks ahead.

"Been out before?" Peta asked.

It happened on almost every transit. Turnover was so high at Luna that transit crew were curious how experienced she was. Kath had never seen Peta on a transit before and thought she could ask the same question. It was just small talk. How are you? Fine weather we're having, etc. Understandable, but it still felt intrusive and uninvited.

"Oh, yeah," Kath replied. "I've been out before." She hoped her tone implied a great deal and didn't offer any more.

"Here is your cabin," Peta said, pointing to door. "I hope you'll like it."

Kath noted the number seven on the door, the only thing setting it apart from the others. They continued the tour.

"Toilet, shower and washing machines," Peta pointed at similar looking doors as she strode past.

She followed Peta down a stair well, through another corridor and doorway, around a bend and into a messroom. Peta pointed at facilities, then down another stairway to the rec room. Exercise room. Cinema. Somehow after the tour of the ship she found herself in front of the door with seven on it. This was the worst part of transit. Everything new and unfamiliar. But it was only temporary.

Kath went into the cabin and felt better in the smaller space. A bunk lined one wall, with a small work cubby that included a desk, monitor and leather chair suitable for launch and work at the station. Light streamed through a porthole, but that would soon be replaced by the dark of space. That was a bonus. Windowless cabins always felt like a prison cell, or a tomb. Even dark was something to look at. Kath lay down on the bunk and closed her eyes. The hum of the warming engines lulled her to sleep until an alarm sounded launch and she strapped into the chair. Peta stuck her head into the door to check she was secure and Kath smiled and held up a thumb. She sat in the plush chair and squeezed the arm rests as the room began to vibrate. Overeating wasn't what really scared her, or boredom. It was always take-off. It typically passed uneventfully.

The wheelhouse offered a good view of Luna. Despite the lack of an actual wheel, the name for the bridge defied time. Steering involved a touch screen. Standing beside the captain, Kath gazed at the distance to the moon. The first mate, John, said she was welcome to visit the bridge, but warned her that although the captain might be brusque to not to take his mood or anything he said too personally. The captain was quiet and Kath reminded herself that silence did not equate to unfriendliness. Years in space could sometimes still the tongue. It was enough that he tolerated her on the bridge.

"Any neighbours today?" she asked.

"Got the gap to ourselves," he said.

"I thought there would be more traffic, more movement to the city." The light of the research station that became the first off planet city could be seen from earth with a small telescope or even a camera with a good zoom lens. She winced as she waited for a gruff response, or none at all.

"They'll be waiting for tighter perigee," he said. His tone made Kath smile and glance his way, almost hopeful for polite conversation.

"In a couple days there will be a lot more traffic," he added. "We add a day leaving early, but the quiet is nice. More junk than ships out here right now, and junk doesn't talk."

She scanned the black and saw nothing, wondering if he just told her to shut up. After several minutes of silence from the captain she thanked him and drifted in the weightlessness back to her cabin.

The ship lurched with a roar, throwing Kath against the straps of her bunk. Releasing herself, she reached and grabbed a handhold as the cabin tilted. She tightened her grip but her hand slipped and she slammed against the bulkhead. The ship was in spin. That shouldn't happen, her stunned brain thought. None of this should happen. An alarm screamed, a continuous wail broadcast over the intercom. Kath's mind tried to interpret its meaning. She struggled to remember the drill, or any of the short safety announcement before launch. It all really meant the same. Get out. She pulled herself to the door and pushed it open, searching for something to grip.

A hand seized her arm and pulled her into the passageway.

"Get to your escape pod!" a crewman shouted. Kath remembered being introduced to the man, but not his name.

"Go!" he shouted again.

She pulled herself to a ladder. She felt hands again, propelling her forward, pushing against her feet and then the backs of her legs. The alarm continued to scream as the ship continued to spin. She reached a hatch at what was the top of the ladder when the ship was on Earth.

"Go! Go! Go!" the person behind her urged.

She felt hot breath on her neck as a body pressed against hers, forcing both of them to the closed door. Words flashed through Kath's mind, painted on steel. Escape Pods. She pushed against the hatch, but it wouldn't budge. Hands reached over her and moved a steel latch. Kath leaned down and pulled at a latch by her feet. A secured door was called 'dogged'. "Doggoned fucking dogged door," was the actual thought that crossed her mind as she yanked on the latch. Metal bit into her flesh, cutting a pattern on her palm, but the door swung open.

"Where's your pod?" the crewman asked.

Kath looked at him blankly. A formality Peta pointed out the first day, lost among myriad details. Muster station. Evacuation pod.

"Never mind," he said, taking her wrist and dragging her towards the pods. Another pair of hands grabbed her free arm and held her.

"Put this on!" she was ordered. Someone thrust an aspirator at her. She put her head through the mask and fumbled with the straps. More hands tightened the strap and connected it to the oxygen cylinder, securing it.

She had done this before, in training, how many years ago? On a sunny day at the swimming pool, in the full gravity of Earth, where they donned the aspirators and oxygen cylinders and jumped into the warm blue water, sitting at the bottom until the instructor indicated they could resurface. Kath looked at the faces around her, blurred by the mask pressing into her face. She heard shouts before understanding dawned. This was not a drill. She remembered more fragments of her training, useless to her now. She was pushed into a pod, into a seat and handed straps. She wriggled into them and tightly fastened all clips.

The pod jerked violently as it ejected from the ship. Her body pressed against its hull as it spun away. The motion made her feel sick, but it slowed before she actually filled the apparatus with the contents of her stomach. Thrusters automatically fired along the outside of the pod, stabilizing its rotation and weightlessness, and helplessness, returned as they drifted.

"You can take that off," a voice told her. Hands reached over and helped pull off her aspirator.

"Breathe normally." Confident, self-assured voice. "Inhale."

Kath gasped and tried to catch her breath, but could not take enough in. She saw the wall mounted straps beside her and remembered she was in an escape pod, the type attached just inside the hull of a ship, used only in extreme emergency. She sucked in air, but for some reason still could not breathe. Strong, familiar hands helped loosen her straps and the pressure on her ribs eased. She took a deep breath, followed by another.

"Are you hurt?" Kath recognized Peta's tanned face starring at hers.

"I ... I don't think so," Kath said.

"Good. Just sit," Peta said before returning to her seat.

"What happened?" Kath asked.

"I don't know," Peta said.

"Something happened in the engine room. An explosion," another passenger, on his way to work on Luna.

"We don't need to know what happened right now," the first mate said. "We just sit tight and await rescue. I'm sure help is already on its way."

"The ship just fucking disappeared."

Kath turned towards the speaker, a young crew member in blue coveralls. Engineering.

"It just ... fucking disappeared."

"Button it," John told him. "Help is on its way. Relax."

Kath looked around the pod. The first mate peered at a device she recognized as an emergency communication terminal. Peta was administering first aid to a crew member's leg. The other passenger wore a grim expression. He looked like a miner. Next to Kath sat the young crewman who spoke about the ship disappearing. His face drained of blood. His hands shook. She recognized the signs of shock from her own first aid training. Everybody working for the company had some level of basic training, some more useful than sitting at the bottom of a swimming pool.

"You were in the engine room?" she asked.

He turned his head and noticed her for the first time, saying nothing.

"What happened down there?" she asked.

"It ... there was a ... I don't know," he answered.

"Are you cold? Let me have your hands," she said.

He offered his hands and Kath rubbed them for want of anything else to do. She remembered physical touch was good to ground a person.

"What's your name?" she asked, keeping hold of a hand when she stopped rubbing.

"Harry," he said.

Kath squeezed his hand. "We're safe now, Harry. Shouldn't be long before help comes, just like John said." She hoped it was true.

The first mate finished tapping at his device, secured it beside him and sat facing the others. Everybody stared at him expectantly. No one spoke. He looked around the small circle and smiled.

"All accounted for," he said. "Other pods are full."

He was greeted with silence. "Who was supposed to be working below?" he asked.

"Me," Harry answered.

"You're a lucky son of a bitch," the first mate said. "Where were you?"

"I was taking a leak," he said.

Laughter spread around the circle of survivors, a release of emotion.

"What the hell happened?" John asked.

"I don't know," he said. "She was purring away as usual, then ..."

"Important thing is we're all here. Just hold tight. This'll be over soon," John said. "Who's thirsty? These have water, and something resembling food."

He dug into a bag under his seat and brought out sachets containing water and energy nutrition bars wrapped in foil. They passed around the pod.

"Eat up. And rest. Might be a long night."

"Give me that first aid kit," Peta said.

The first mate floated it across the pod to her and she caught it in her lap. She fished out a heat pad, activated it and placed it on the leg of the crewman next to her. The first mate secured the bag of supplies and unwrapped an energy bar. Kath sucked on hers, trying to soften it enough to chew while she watched the crew member being administered to.

"Minding accounts and answering calls," her mother had chided. "That's called a secretary. You don't have to go to the moon to do that."

"Maybe, mom, but the pay is nowhere as good as it is up there." Kath's usual response. Tied down to an office at just above minimum wage, she'd never have time to sail and never get out of the bank's death pledge. That's what a mortgage is, she told her mother. Mort. Gage. Death Pledge. Pledging my life to the bank, til to death do us part.

"You can have a home here and not have to do that. You father and I had a mortgage and we paid it off," her mother argued. "I worry so when you're up there."

"You don't have to worry mom." Does she have to do this every time? "And it was different for you and dad! After my time up there I'll be a home owner. That's something very few of my friends can say."

Now for the put down.

"That's not a home. It's tiny. You can hardly move around in it. And it can sink. Then what would you have?"

"I'd have an insurance pay out." Kath's unsatisfactory reply. She understood her mother's concern, but that generation just didn't understand what it was like in the real world.

Still, Kath thought as she sat in pod, maybe she'd find another job as soon as she could, when they were rescued and returned to Earth. It would take longer to pay off the boat, but ... She caught the first mate's eye. What did he read in hers?

"We'll get out of here," he said quietly. "Help will come soon."

She nodded. The pod continued to drift away from the wreckage of the spaceship. Harry chewed slowly on his nutrician bar. Kath closed her eyes and let the sounds around lull her into an exhausted sleep.

Kath awoke to a jolt. The pod vibrated, then was still. The others roused and looked around the small craft as confused as she. The sound of metal grinding against metal drew all eyes to the hatch. They watched as it slowly opened. A man peered through at them.

"What a ride, huh?" he said. "But it's over now. Follow me. Welcome to the *Nineteen*."

Confused faces stared back. "You're okay now," he said. "Follow me." He disappeared back into the hatch.

He was replaced by another stranger. "Come, take my hand," he said. He reached into the escape pod, waiting for any taker.

John took it and was hauled out of pod. The others followed. They entered a brightly lit corridor.

Kath trailed the feet in front of her as they drifted to a larger room. It was a mess room. A medic checked them one at a time. They were offered sachets of coffee and a paste of sugar and dough in a tube. Kath read the label on the tube and giggled. Coffee and donuts.

A man dressed like a captain appeared after they had finished and introduced himself. "I'm Captain Young," he said. "You're on the *Calipso Nineteen*, transit to Luna. You're all safe now and we'll get you to base on time."

Silence sat in room heavier than the absence of gravity allowed.

"The other pods?" John asked, his words falling heavily through weightlessness.

"They're fine," the man replied. "They're all accounted for. Picked up by a transit returning to Earth. But you're the lucky ones. We'll have you on base and to work on time. I'm afraid quarters will be cramped, but we'll make do."

"Thanks," John said. "We really appreciate your help."

Kath sucked the remainder of her donut and disappointedly clutched an empty sachet of coffee. A crew member touched her shoulder, noticed the crumbled drink sachet and gave her another, full and warm. She thanked her, toothed open the cap and sucked in the warm black medicine.

"We'll be at Luna before you know it," the crew member said. "Get you to work on time."

Kath smiled, not really meaning it. But she pushed that aside. She'd spend the next three months on Luna fulfilling her contract and be that much closer to owning her boat. Her home.

"Thank you," Kath said.

on THe Lam

"So why do you want to space?" Standard questions. The man interviewing me sat behind a desk large enough to be called a table.

"I want to use my skills where I can, and develop into the best officer I can," Blah blah, et cetera, et cetera.

"You're not applying for an officer's position," the man said.

"I'm only making my goals transparent," I answered.

"I don't think very much here is transparent," he said.

"I'm not sure I know ..."

"No, um," he looked at my dossier again. "Mr. Jensen. I think you do. Tell me, your skipper lost at sea, an investigation underway, and you want to leave the planet. Clarify."

Sweat formed under my arms and began to trickle down my side. It helped keep me focused. "A man has to eat, and to eat he needs work," I said. "Besides, the pickings are getting slim out there. It's a dying industry."

"True about that," the man replied. "This file tells the story of a rather unpleasant relationship. You didn't like your skipper much, did you?"

"I think that feeling was mutual," I answered. "But while we sailed, professionalism overrode petty feelings." It was pure bullshit. The man across the table smelled it.

"Bullshit," the man across from me said.

"Okay," I admitted. "He was an insecure little megalomaniac. He didn't like initiative, and if you got too good at your job, he felt threatened. Sure, I didn't like him, but when we were at sea, I worked for him—"

"You thought you could do his job better."

"Yeah, I did," I said.

"And he is lost at sea and you skipper the scow home. Funny that," he said.

"If I wanted to skipper that ship, I wouldn't be here right now; I'd be applying for his job. You have the reports. As soon as I noticed the skipper was missing, I followed protocol, and we did everything in our power to search ..."

To search for him, after I went to my bunk for four hours to stare at the ceiling, let a lot of nautical miles pass beneath us, before climbing back on deck and sounding the alarm.

Usually the wind would blow the smell of rotting fish away. Some of the crew wore foam plugs stuffed up their nostrils. Soak the foam in essential oils, vinegar, anything. I never bothered, just like Skipper never bothered. It was some sort of macho challenge, or test, or game the skipper played. Oh, how he liked his games.

Fish were getting scarce as we grabbed everything we could from the depths. We set the net, dredged the bottom for the little treasures, and increasingly hauled up garbage. Fish with names like 'rat', 'hag', 'toad', because they were, and worth about as much. We emptied the net of the slimy garbage and reset, sending it down again, not bothering too much with clean up. Skipper was a lot of things, and slob was one of them. I hated how he kept the ship as much as I hated him. But I had a job, and those were getting as scarce as the fish we chased, further and further from shore.

"All he wants is loyalty." That was Rogers, a newer crew member. What a strange interaction. I don't remember why he said that. Probably overhearing me mumble about the stench of a dirty ship.

"He doesn't know what that word means." A dangerous moment of honesty. I didn't know or trust Rogers yet.

"Just serve the boat, stay true to mission," Rogers said. "And he'll take us places."

I looked at him, trying to decide if he was an acolyte, or just naïve.

"He doesn't want loyalty, he wants submission," I said. As long as you rolled on your back and presented your belly to the alpha dog, your cruise would be bearable. But show a little initiative, a bit of independent thinking, a trace of a spine, and the games would begin.

"He's just a bully with a massive insecurity complex. He's not going to take you anywhere." That was too far, and the look from Rogers told me I might as well as said it to the boss himself. But I felt a weight lift from my shoulders, realizing I finally didn't care anymore. This would be my last voyage, and probably my last paycheck for quite a while.

"Jensen, what the fuck do you call this!" Stormy now, days after from that interaction with Rogers. Swell at four meters, wind gusting at sixty knots. Skipper shouting in my face, spittle mixed with rain. Line was strewn across the deck, coils that weren't secured properly. I didn't do it, but it was somebody on my watch, so I am responsible.

Probably Rogers, getting back at me for disrespecting his skipper. Even if the toilet blocked up, it was the Watch Captain's fault, and the Watch Captain would clean it up. Skipper would see to that, especially if it happened on my watch. I wouldn't be surprised if Skipper saved up his turds and emptied himself during my six hours on deck, complete with a few rolls of toilet paper to make sure it would clog and overflow. I was actually his most experienced crew member, something that caused even more resentment.

"You're fucking worthless, Jensen! Get this mess secured."

The ship rode the waves, just as it was designed. I bent my knees and stood on the deck as if it were at its mooring, perfectly balanced. The sky darkened. A squall. Skipper staggered forward in protest of my inaction. He grabbed a line for support and shouted in my face.

"Get your worthless ass moving and clean up my deck!"

I stood, knees flexed, riding the deck, up, down. Rain drenched us. I squinted my eyes to stop the water from blinding me. Sunburnt face in front of mine.

One thing Skipper had taught me that I actually found useful was that the most important thing to have on board any ship, and on your body at all times, was a sharp knife. That nugget of advice came early in our relationship, when I was still an obedient little pup.

Sheets of rain. Up. Down. A wave crashed over the railing and Skipper lost his footing, slipped to his knees. But he didn't lose his grip. He pulled himself upright. My feet seemed bolted to the deck. Another wave smashed over the railing. By the time Skipper steadied himself, I had my knife out. The look on his face ... it'll never go away, an image I can never share with others.

Confusion. Anger. Rage. But not pain, no, not pain. Skipper would never show that. That would show weakness, and he had to show he wasn't weak, even when he was dying and it didn't matter anymore. I drove the blade in again. Skipper's eyes widened. His grimace grew more ominous. I drove the blade in a third time. I left the knife in Skipper's ribs and grabbed his coat at the shoulders. I dragged my captain to the railing and unceremoniously pushed him over. I didn't hear a splash. I didn't even bother to look back. Instead, I turned my attention to the deck and started coiling and securing the loose line.

"Yeah, it's all here," the man said, closing the file. "You followed protocol to the letter. Looks neat and tidy. I also have testimonials. I would suggest re-considering some of your references in your next application."

"And I'm sure you can't tell me who they might be," I said.

The man opposite pursed his lips and shook his head.

"But you could tell me who gave me a good one. And why I'm sitting here now." I already knew, but played like I didn't. I called him as soon as we reached land, the only person I knew that might be able to help. He obviously could.

"You know who. He's a good man, and I trust his judgment. But we also have an informal network, and I have to listen to that too."

"It's a small community," I said. The ocean was big, the crews that work on it aren't. "That doesn't surprise me. And what does this informal network say of me?"

"It says you have a problem with hierarchy. That doesn't bode well when you're on a ship, light-years from Earth," he said.

"Fair enough. I admit I have a problem with *bad* hierarchy, but not with discipline on a ship," I said, realizing my mistake too late.

"Yes, Mr. Jensen." He leaned back in the chair and took a long look at me. "Working on a space freighter isn't the picnic a fishing boat is. There's no view, for one. You're locked in a lead-lined shoebox for months on end. You'll need to start at the bottom when it comes to piloting and walking. But like I said—months in a shoebox is plenty of time to train. You're lucky, Mr. Jensen.".

I knew enough to know when to speak and when to keep quiet. I kept quiet.

"We're a little short of competent crew at the moment. We have a ship that lost a couple of crew members quite recently. Something involving law enforcement, and them not being able to leave the planet for a few years. Besides, it seems that shipping has lost a bit of its luster, and those willing to spend years of their lives transporting settlers and supplies to far-flung rocks are getting hard to come by. And I can tell you, you'll be going *pretty* far. Wipe that smile off your face."

His tone grew hard. "I'm giving you this job because of our mutual acquaintance. He said you were competent, and he said you were trustworthy. My god, you better not prove him wrong. He also said I still owed him one, nothing you need to know about, and giving you this ticket would clear our slate."

He stood up and reached across the table. I took his hand and bit down as he squeezed tight.

"I like your Captain. She's good at her job," he said. "Do not give her any grief. If you do, and if you ever set foot earthside again, you won't be walking much farther." He let go of my hand.

"Shuttle leaves 0600 tomorrow. I'm sure you'll be on it," he said. "Go straight to the *Cirrus* and check-in. She's your new home. And close the door behind you."

I was strapped into my seat by 0530, watching the door of the shuttle and only starting to relax when it closed for take-off. I felt pushed into the cushions as the craft sped down the runway and took off, banking for its long spiral to launch height of eighty thousand feet.

When the time came for the final push into space, I copied those next to me, leaning my head fully against the back of my seat. The force of the thrusters sat on my chest like a fully-grown gorilla, pounding its fists on my temples for good measure. I strained to see out the port, but the shuddering of the shuttle blurred my vision, and it was enough to just keep breathing.

And then the beast ceased its attack. I sucked air into my lungs now that they were free of gravity. I felt my body float upwards, held in place by the straps on my seat. I reached for the bag in the pocket on the back of the seat in front of me, opened it quickly and vomited. I folded it closed so that the contents of my stomach wouldn't float around the cabin.

So, this was freefall.

The shuttle adjusted position, and a slight kick to my back signaled a push towards the space hub. Halfway to the destination, the shuttle slowly flipped and kicked again, this time decelerating. Docking was so smooth I didn't feel it. I unstrapped when the intercom announced it was okay and tried to show the caution it advised. I hit the ceiling, attempted to correct my flight, and was pushed back into my seat. I held the armrest tightly to stop my momentum and tried again, moving from handhold to handhold, keeping one hand gripped to something not moving.

Icons on the docking bay exit instructed passengers to ensure their feet were facing downward as they entered the port's artificial gravitation. I managed to maintain my balance and stepped onto the moving walkway, letting it carry me into the hub. Here was at least a bit of familiarity. From space the port resembled a bike tire with its rim removed, thin spokes sticking out from a central hub, and at the end of each spoke was a docking bay. The interior of the hub looked like any large airport on earth. I studied the monitors until I found the spoke

I needed, saw I had several hours to wait, and located a bar next to a large viewport.

Selecting the most expensive single malt whiskey on offer, I ordered a double. I took a sip like a condemned man enjoying his last meal, and gazed down at the most beautiful and rich planet in the known universe. The blue expanse of the Pacific lay below me. I tried not to suppress the emotion I was feeling. I wanted to at least acknowledge it. Loss? Regret? I spent most of the last five years of my life on the water, with an uninterrupted horizon that circled my entire world. The colors of sunrise. Clouds towering in the distance or exploding with blinding light right overhead. I let myself get lost in memories.

I lifted my glass and noticed it was empty, as well as that hours had passed as I watched my previous life pass beneath. I made my way down a spoke to my gate where a much smaller shuttle waited to take me to the ship. Stepping into freefall through the departure gate, I managed to keep the whiskey inside and found a seat. The shuttle detached and a brief blast from the engines propelled it away. I watched the ship grow from a speck of distant light to an ugly freighter. It held a precious cargo: building supplies, seed, fertilizer, solar panels and energy cells. Everything needed to build a new world. It even carried settlers, who believed a barren and empty rock in a far-flung corner of the galaxy could bring a better future.

As the shuttle neared, I stared out the porthole at the *Cirrus*. One thing was certain, calling these ships 'shoeboxes' was complimentary. It was more like the containers loaded onto the cargo ships that plied the Earth's oceans. Rectangular metal hunks devoid of any individuality or character. The only way to differentiate bow from stern was the fusion reactors that propelled it. Of course, when it came time to decelerate the ship would flip, and the stern become the bow. Was that called 'shunting' back on ancient Earth? In space, there was no up or down, so it probably didn't matter if a ship had a front or back.

I wondered about this new home, a container ship with a nuclear reactor in it. Will I ever feel the water all around my body again? I thought. Swim in the sea? Breathe fresh air? Be drowned by rain while on watch?

It didn't matter. It was too late for regrets. I made my choice, and I burnt my bridge.

PSYCHONAUT

"Have you completed your preparations?"

The question seems merely routine as she is tucking me into the bed. Kind of a bed. It is one of those mechanical ones that adjusted to whatever position the user wants. This one is horizontal, mostly, but raised a bit at the head so I won't need a lot of pillows. Because that's how I want it. It is the only bed in the room. A small table stands beside with a lamp on it. Yellow curtains stop any light from outside entering the sacred space, yet allow enough to give a glow of sunrise. Imagine the type of room in a nice hospital where a woman gives birth. Ambient lighting, all that.

"Tell me your preparations," she says. Commands. Asks. Whatever. She is by the book, which actually makes me feel better. Relaxed. Safe.

"I meditated before coming," I say, knowing that isn't enough.

"And describe your meditation."

"I practiced mindfulness for thirty minutes," I reply.

"What does that mean to you?" she asks.

I smile. She was thorough, but rather than annoyed I feel relieved. I wanted to be among people who knew what they doing, and who took it seriously.

"I, um, concentrated on my breath, you know, watching it go in, and watching it go out."

"How did you find that?" she asks.

"Frustrating," I admit. "But, you know, back to the task at hand."

"And did it help to still your mind?"

"Eventually. I think the trick is in not kicking yourself, you know? The mind wanders, the mind wanders, it's just what it's been trained to do."

"That's very perceptive," she says as she swabs the inside of my arm with something smelling of ammonia. "It's called monkey mind. Jumping from thought to thought. Limb to limb."

"Thank you. That's a good analogy," I reply.

"And after your mindfulness meditation, what was your mantra?"

We were told or requested or given the idea that a mantra was important, that it would help focus the mind and guide our experience. I might bullshit about most things, like about how productive sitting and observing my breath for thirty minutes might be, but for some reason I couldn't help being nakedly honest for this part.

"I said," I say. "Let me stand on the edge of the unknown and fall into the abyss, accepting whatever might occur."

I feel a pinch as a needle is inserted into my arm and my skin stretches as the cannula is taped on. She hooks up the IV but didn't open the drip yet.

"Repeat that," she says.

"What?"

"Repeat your mantra. It's very good."

"Let me stand on the edge of the unknown and fall into the abyss, accepting whatever might occur."

"Again," she demands. "Say it again."

"Let me stand on the edge of the unknown and fall into the abyss, accepting whatever might occur."

She opens the drip. I feel her hand on my forehead. Her breath close to my face. I want to touch her, though I have no reason, except maybe comfort, a way to hold on. And I want her to touch me, because I am a little scared. But she doesn't touch me. Instead, time stops. I stop. She stops. The world ceases to exist, at least in any form recognized by the majority of humanity going about their daily lives. Despite the solution being injected into my vein and not into my mouth, I feel the familiar taste in the back of my throat. No, not a taste, but a sensation. A pressing, a grating. Okay, a definite taste, but only of the drug.

I've bonged loads of DMT before, and this is the initial sensation every time. I say initial, because it is momentary, fragmentary, instantaneous. I describe taking DMT as a psychedelic sledgehammer slamming into your frontal cortex. I slap my forehead when talking to a friend. Like that, I say. Slap! You are away. You can fight it, spend the whole time saying, "Oh no, I don't want this!" Or you can open yourself to the fifteen minutes of multidimensional travel that expensive little hit will give you.

But this is different. I'm not on my couch in the living room, bong loaded and lighter ready. I didn't sign up for a fifteen-minute trip to the cosmos. I volunteered for hours. Hours. DMT is classed as a Schedule One drug under the controlled substances act. That classification dates back to Nixon, if that tells you anything about attitudes. Those conservative fuckers were scared. Capital 'S' scared. Especially with anything that enabled the user to experience a reality different than the monochrome pictures displayed on their television screens. LSD, marijuana, mushrooms, peyote. Aside from acid, the others are natural. Mother nature showing the way. I always say, follow the lady. In whatever shape she may take. Make that a mantra. Mother Nature Knows. Follow Her.

Laws are catching up, and most substances are legal in any state I'd want to visit. And research programs like the one I am involved in are being approved. But *N, N-Dimethyltryptamine* remains a very misunderstood demon. I use that description sarcastically, of course. That's how the legislators who designate classifications must feel about it—a demon or devil. Or they have simply no experience or understanding of its gifts. I prefer to default to the kinder option of thinking that they really have no fucking idea about what they are doing and how much pain they are causing to actual human beings with their stupid laws. DMT is called the 'spirit molecule' for a reason. It's in all of us, released by the pineal gland at birth and death, guiding us into new realities. Opening the third eye. If our brains are computers, DMT is the reboot. Helping to write an entirely new program.

I'm all for that.

Laws or classifications never stopped people from doing drugs. They never will. Obviously. We want to escape, or we need to escape. Which, I think, is a sad excuse to do drugs. It plays into their fucking plan. Rather than overthrow the corrupt system (power to the people, there's a hell of a lot more of us than the one percent) people freebase or shoot up heroin or smoke themselves numb with something else. If that were a real solution, they'd hand out Xbox 8 or 9-s or 10-s or 19-s and we can play computer games all the day long. And shit, that's what we're doing. Computer games. TikTok. Facebook. ABC. NBC. Netflix. Amazon. Hulu. Whatever. Distraction.

Do you get it now? Using drugs should be to open the doors of perception. That's Aldous Huxley, not the cool band who named themselves after the book. The Doors. Jim Morrison. Light My Fire. We've all heard them. I'm talking about *doors* of *perception* and *opening* them. And you don't have to tell me you haven't read Huxley yet, because I know you haven't. If you have, welcome aboard.

I repeat my mantra, though I don't even know if it escaped my mouth. "Let me stand on the edge of the unknown and fall into the abyss, accepting whatever might occur." I say it to myself or anybody near, though she is already far and away. I was lucky to hear about the trial. Or maybe not just lucky—I looked long and hard for a study like this one. And I was accepted, and here I am. A psychonaut, exploring the great within. Not inhaling a fifteen-minute hit of DMT, but accepting it intravenously for a twelve-hour voyage. I don't wear a space suit and zoom through the cosmos in a metal ship. I lay on a reclining bed with a needle in my vein, drip fed a magical solution, gift of mother nature and some clever scientists. But I am travelling through more than space.

DMT is typically smoked because the body has a way of cancelling out its power if taken orally. That's why a monoamine oxidase inhibitor is needed to prolong the voyage. Without those fancy sounding words, the body negates the effect if taken orally, unlike with a mushroom or a tab of acid. The body doesn't seem to mind those. But with DMT it's a little different. Maybe it's the body's way of keeping us attached to one reality so we can feed it and keep it breathing. It's also why indigenous people in the Amazon added other plants to their brews. Think ayahuasca. They knew about monoamine oxidase inhibitors. Some say they knew because the plants told them. I like that. I'm sure the researchers or professors leading this study learned from those folks in the Amazon before synthesizing their own formula.

I feel the familiar grating at the back of my mouth, far back in the pallet that always escapes description, as the drug enters my system.

"Let me stand on the edge of the unknown and fall into the abyss, accepting whatever might occur."

Her hand rests on my forearm. She gives it a light squeeze. Then she removes her hand. Or I just can't feel anything in that particular temporal realm anymore.

I hear them singing. It is like the tinkling of broken crystal, as it is breaking again and again, but with purpose. Deliberate. Orchestrated. A symphony beyond my understanding. My vision is filled with colors and shapes, as if I am inside one of those tubes we looked through as kids. Kaleidoscopes. But like the music, there is a purpose, a symmetry, but I can't understand it. I watch the rotation of the geometric patterns and listen to the sounds. They are singing to me, I think. And I remember my mantra. To fall into the abyss. Beyond visual and even aural sensation. What is beyond the geometry and symphony? I wait. I watch.

And then I feel a grating, as if metal shutters were grinding closed. Colors become grey. Sounds become a groan. And then all is gone. I open my eyes, close them again, blink rapidly, until the light of the room becomes acceptable.

"They took my memory," I say without thinking. And I feel that they have. Whatever or wherever I had been, was gone. But why did I say 'they'?

I feel a hand on my arm. "Tell me." My guide. Research assistant. Spiritual doula. Whatever she is.

"I don't know," I say. It isn't quite a lie. I can't articulate the feeling. "What happened?" I ask. "That was too short."

"You travelled for hours." She tells me.

"No way." I stare at her, waiting for her to tell me she is joking. But she doesn't.

"What did you mean, 'they took your memory?'" she asks.

And instead of answering her, I cry softly. I close my moist eyes and lay back. I want to wipe my eyes but I have no hands and I have no eyes. I am immersed in black, filled only with a faint and distant tinkling of breaking crystal. I follow the sound, focusing all my attention on the aural sensation. I realize my intention is wrong. It is too bound in the self, far too egotistical for journeying in a place with no-self. I shorten my mantra and repeated it silently.

"Let me." It is more a plea than anything else.

I listen.

And I feel a breeze, I feel the breath of the person standing above my body. I feel the warmth of the air against my skin. Each separate particle, each mote of matter, strikes my skin, wave after wave of matter, like wind against a sail propelling a boat across the sea, it pushes and guides me. And I realized that all mater is a wave. Everything. Light. Gravity. Me. I am a wave. Just a wave of matter, tiny particles, flowing through the cosmos. It's not too hard to imagine. A wave of water is solid, watch it lap against the shore, but looking closer it is merely molecules of hydrogen and oxygen bound together. Peer even closer and those dissolve into miniscule units. The ocean ceases to exist as ocean, water ceases to exist as water. Where are these thoughts coming from? Thought is a wave! Dissect each bubble and examine its true nature. Time is a wave! Made up of microscopic particles, each buffeting me and joining me as I travel. And I begin to see them, tiny particles of time, as I grow smaller or larger or ...

They are teaching me.

I focus on the many particles I am immersed among, although I can't quite identify a 'me'. I am mere observer. My attention falls upon one mere spec, a meager dot. The more I focus, the larger it grows, the more minuscule I become, and I fall into it. I open my eyes. I blink rapidly, until the light of the room becomes acceptable.

I feel a hand on my arm. "Tell me." My guide. Research assistant. Spiritual doula. Whatever he is.

"I think I'm lost," I say

"What happened?" he asks.

I am in the only bed in the room. A small table stands beside it with a lamp on it. Pink curtains stop any light from outside entering the sacred space, yet allow enough to give a glow of sunset.

I look from him to my arm, the needle taped to my skin. I look past it to my wrist, my upturned palm, my fingers. My eyes continue their journey across all the lines to my small finger, my pinky, and then to its tip. The skin is smooth, filled only with the spirals of my print. One of my earliest memories is my small hand placed on the dash of our neighbor's car. My mother didn't drive, not since she was involved in an accident that killed others in the vehicle they drove and almost killed me and my brother and sister. For the rest of her life, she never drove again. That accident must have happened very shortly before mine. I only realize that now. My poor mother.

That is why the neighbor is driving. There is a cloth under my hand, but it is red, soaked with my blood. A little hand, placed on the dash, making a mess of the neighbor's car. That is the memory. I have others, from a little later. A hospital visit, stiches removed, scabs around the scar, more snap shots burned into a very young boy's synapses, or however memory is made.

My mother was Hispanic, so when we watched television, she taught us to honor Tonto instead of that racist white savior he rode with, The Lone Ranger. He was never alone, really, was he? He always had his brown friend watching his back. And of course Zorro was the man. The hand on the dash wasn't actually my first memory of the accident. My brother and I were playing sword fighting. I remember that too, if only as a glimpse. I don't know who was Zorro that day. Maybe we both were. I took my sister's twirling baton, the type cheerleaders use, and used it for my foil. The rubber end was missing, as they always are, and I stuck my little finger into it to help my small hand grip it better. That's not really a memory, just an older me figuring out what I did. Then lunge, faint, riposte, parry, as only a three and five year could do.

My older brother must have hit that baton really hard to severe the tip of my finger. Really hard. I only realize that now.

But the tip of the pinky I see at the end of my hand has no scar. I stare at the uninterrupted swirls making a print that no other human in the planet has in just the same way. Then I look at my guide. Research assistant. Spiritual doula. Whatever he is. He looks very familiar. I remember him asking me how I prepared, being very 'by-the-book', as he was taught. Because academic rigor was important in a scientific experiment. I remember feeling safe, relaxed. Only I don't feel relaxed now. I feel an itch at the back of my soul telling me that something isn't right. Or that everything is right, but I am not. He is supposed to say something. Or I am. But I don't know what I am supposed to say. Did I want to touch him?

It is too much to take in, so I close my eyes. And I hear them singing. It is like the tinkling of broken crystal, as if it were cracking again and again, but with purpose. Deliberate. Orchestrated. The sound is a wave, and I join it. I become it. And among all the particles or photons or quarks or bosons or whatever name they're given, I flow across the universe. I let my attention expand to what I am among, what I am, because although separate, if you zoom out from all the little ripples, of all the realities, we are all one wave. And like the sea as it heaves and flows over the earth, it is made of hundreds, thousands, millions, trillions, of tiny droplets.

My focus rests on a small piece of reality, one of the many small dewdrops of being, and I enter it.

I feel a hand on my arm. My guide. Research assistant. Spiritual doula. Whatever she is. I am in the only bed in the room. A small table stands beside the bed with a lamp on it. Green curtains stop any light from outside entering the sacred space, yet allow enough light to give a glow of spring, of new life. I only glance at my guide's familiar face, focusing instead at my arm where the needle penetrates, and to my wrist and palm and fingers. I stare at the missing tip of my little finger. I was sword fighting with my brother. It was one of my earliest memories. I stuck my pinky into the end of my sister's twirling baton, the type cheerleaders use and that little girls that are encouraged by a society to cheer from the sidelines want for Christmas. He must have hit it really hard to severe the tip of my finger. I bled all over the dash of my neighbor's car on the way to the hospital.

"Tell me." My guide. Research assistant. Spiritual doula. Whatever she was. It is her job to collect data for the project.

"I don't know," I say. It isn't quite a lie. "I've been here before. I think."

I close my eyes hard. Tinkling incomprehensible music fills my ears. I drift in a wave of time, a sea of worlds, many worlds, a wave of photons and quarks and bosons or whatever name they're given, searching for my way home. Each one a world, each one a home. But only one that is mine.

AGENT WILLS GOES UNDERCOVER

Agent Rebecca Wills sat on a bench overlooking the children's playground. A father pushed his daughter on a swing. She giggled as he made a funny noise each time he sent her into the air. A boy cried beside the sand pit and his mother stepped over to comfort him. She picked up his plastic toy truck and played with him for a few moments before he was happy enough for her to return to her takeaway coffee and resume her chat with a friend. A dog yelped, stretching the lead that tied him to the fence as a squirrel hurried up a nearby tree.

"Apricot glow," Wills said, turning her eyes to the horizon. It came out as speculation.

The woman sitting next to Wills stopped fingering the screen of her phone and set the device on the bench between them. Her phone recorded everything that was said. But Wills didn't say anymore until she received confirmation.

"A beautiful light," the woman next to her replied.

It was always somebody different and in a different location. Wills suggested the park. Open, populated. A natural place for two women to strike up a conversation while the children played. And there was no trace aside from the recording the other agent would take back to the field office. Nothing could be found, no manila envelopes with case notes, no photos or laptop or cell phone. Her apartment remained clean, her identity secure. At least the identity the Bureau created for her.

"I haven't slept well," Wills said. More cloak and dagger stuff. "It's hard getting used to a new bed." This part was to verify who was speaking on the recording. It said: This is Rebecca Wills of the Federal Bureau of Investigation submitting my report.

"I always have strange dreams when I stay at a hotel," the woman answered. Acknowledged. There wasn't an agreed script. Sleep and dream were the key words.

"I'm still making beds and cleaning toilets," Wills said, watching the father continue to push his daughter. "Dormitory and ablutions. They take hygiene very seriously. All attendant's shower before start-ing a shift, put clothes into lockers and change into grey scrubs. No way to smuggle a button camera, wire, or obtain any physical evidence. Not even underwear is allowed. The inmates follow a similar practice. Every morning they change into a clean gown and wash themselves in ablutions. They are all non-verbal, but so are the attendants. I haven't heard a word exchanged, inmates or attendants. Just basic signs and facial gestures. The inmates make and understand these signs, even manage a very limited conversation. I am fine. I am happy. I will eat now. That kind of thing. And they all learn and follow their individual routines, so there's intelligence there, of a sort."

Wills stood, took a step forward and retrieved an errant ball. She returned to the bench after rolling it back to a child.

"Some of the women are pregnant," she continued. "One started labor while I was on shift. Her water broke and she was taken into the clinic. I haven't seen inside the clinic yet. I haven't seen inside many other rooms. Routine reigns supreme and there isn't much opportunity to stray. From stepping on the bus to the center and back, it's all very tightly regulated."

Wills watched the action in the playground and the agent next to her described the tree shading a corner of the sand pit. It was easier and more realistic than just making movements with her mouth. From a distance it looked like the equal give and take of normal conversation. But they had been talking long enough.

The agent next to Wills picked up her phone when she finished with the tree. "There seems to be a bit of a chill in the evenings," she observed. Are you secure?

"I don't feel it," Wills replied. "I've always liked the autumn." I am fine.

"Your apartment is being watched, so be careful," the woman said as she rose, dispensing with secret words. She placed her phone in her purse and strode off.

"As far as I can tell, all the women inmates are exactly the same," Wills said. They had run through the usual verifications. The phone between her and the man sitting on the stool at the diner was conveniently placed between them. It picked up her voice clearly and the clatter of dishes and food cooking were mere background.

"Like there is one model they're all copied from. The same goes for the males. All the same. I'd speculate that they're clones, if that's at all possible. Differences come from what is done to them. When they change in the morning it is all in plain sight. They have absolutely no compunction about being naked in front of each other. They don't even seem to notice. But I have seen some with large scars across their sides, like a kidney donor scar, or a C-Section. Some women have obvious stretch marks. Some inmates are missing an eye. Others wear bandages, typically on the inside of an arm. Just a hunch, but it's like they're a one stop shop for body parts. Until I can get into the clinic that's only conjecture."

She took a sip of her iced tea. What she saw in the center shocked her, but she repressed any feelings and continued to play the role of care attendant simply doing a job. Everybody there acted the same. She wanted to speak to a co-worker outside, off the bus, when life took on a semblance of normality, but each worker got off at a different stop. And like inside the center, speaking on the bus was forbidden.

The man next to her finished talking about his hamburger meat being undercooked, almost cold. She replied with a comment about hers being fine and ended her report.

She put a twenty-dollar bill under her glass for her meal and a tip and left. She stepped out into the late afternoon sun, pausing momentarily to let its warmth soak into her skin. Federal Agent Rebecca Wills didn't exist out here. Ronda Galanis, care attendant for Benedict Health Solution, did and walked the half mile to her house. It wasn't the type of place Rebecca would have chosen. But Ronda didn't have much choice. The rent was affordable, and the landlord didn't mind if she hung pictures on the walls. There were a lot of pictures. An older couple that were her parents. A woman somewhat resembling Ronda, a sister. Beside her were several of Ronda's make-believe nieces and nephews. There were pictures of Greek islands and dry, rugged mountains. Ronda had dreams of visiting one day, exploring the family homeland.

She closed and locked the door behind her, went to the refrigerator and took out the remains of a bottle of white wine. She filled a glass, left the empty bottle on the counter, and sat on the couch gazing at the black screen of the television. Both Ronda and Rebecca were lonely in the small house. But it was what they signed up for. Volunteered. Wills helped create Ronda so she knew her well, like her tendency to drink when she felt this way. Rebecca had the same problem. At least there was something they had in common.

Wills woke long before the sun, dressed, ate a bowl of cereal, and made her way to the bus stop. She learned through simple hand gestures that her shift had been changed. You are being transferred to Laundry Services. Report to work at four am. She signed in response that she understood. Wills would have liked to have had her service revolver with her on the walk to the bus stop but made do with a small can of mace she held in one hand the whole way. Ronda couldn't afford a safer neighborhood. But there was no need. She saw a car down the street with two shadows within. They could be agents, or they could be from BHS. Or they could be two people sitting in a car at four in the morning that didn't care who Ronda Galanis or Rebecca Wills was. She doubted the latter and would ask at the next debrief.

Wills boarded the bus. Twelve co-workers already sat silently. Some looked up as she entered but most ignored her. The bus stopped ten more times before reaching the gate, the only entrance to the sprawling compound consisting of one massive warehouse-like structure surrounded by a tall fence. A guard boarded and checked the driver's identification. She held hers up, as did the others. He walked down the aisle briefly checking each, turned, and then exited. Agent Wills worked in laundry for three months. She ran the industrial washing and drying machines as they processed bed sheets, gowns, scrubs, towels, any fabric used at the center. When they were dry, she folded most and pressed others. She used muscle rub on her sore lower back and moisturizing cream on her dry and chapped hands. Her reports were brief, mostly estimates of the center's population. The laundry she processed fit the amount of beds in the dormitory, as the number of gowns matched the inmate population. She was reminded that all the details she provided contributed to creating a fuller picture of the operation. Her work was appreciated. The car wasn't theirs. Was she feeling okay, did she have a cold? (Do you feel in danger?) No, the house is well heated.

Wills returned to her small rental every night, or early morning, or afternoon depending on her shift. Sometimes she thought she saw a car, but she wasn't sure. BHS had a strict non-disclosure policy. It probably seemed reasonable to those employed—steady pay, salary scale to climb, benefits and pension. Just don't ever, ever, talk about what you do. Half of her job interview seemed taken up with that, and the consequences should work be discussed away from work, and with any person not employed by BHS. They wouldn't need too many people in cars near an employee's house to send a message about how much the company cares. Isn't that the most efficient form of surveillance, make sure the employees felt they were being watched all the time, even if they weren't? That way they begin to watch themselves.

The cashiers at the liquor store started to greet Ronda by name as she stopped on the way home and bought a bottle or two of white wine. Two, if she were being honest. It helped, or so she pretended, sitting on her sofa alone and staring at the black screen. She turned the device on from time to time but the drivel coming out of made her angry and she always turned it off again. It was why Rebecca didn't have a television in the apartment she hadn't seen in months. She would have to try very hard to break the practice of self-medicating with alcohol if this assignment ever ended.

Then Ronda, or Attendant Forty-Eight as she was referred to at the center, was transferred to physiotherapy. She helped inmates with their post-operative rehabilitation programs, made sure others had everything they needed to pursue their individual fitness programs, and noted any exercise machines in need of repair. Most of her role seemed supervisory. There, if needed by an inmate, and to assist the personal trainers if required. But she saw more than she did in the laundry. Most inmates appeared in optimal physical condition. They circulated from machine to machine, working legs, arms, back, abdomen, lungs, hearts. Wills placed their age at mid-twenties. The peak of youth. She wished she looked as good at the same age, and she was academy fit at that time of her life.

She interacted more with the inmates, albeit through gestures. She was amazed at the differing personalities lurking within such similar bodies. Number Thirty-One had a dry sense of humor and could play out a joke with two hands and expressive eyebrows. Laughter was with bent wrists and twitching, cupped hands. Number One-Eighty-One was best avoided. Even male attendants gave him and his strange sexual energy as wide a berth as their work permitted. Fifty-Two seemed genuinely concerned with the wellbeing of others. Wills tried asking innocuous questions. Both hands in front of her torso, then raise to show two thumbs. Are you okay? A point and a swipe of hand over mouth. Are you happy? Answers were affirmative or directed toward specific injury. She bent a finger and then pointed away and tried other gestures. Do you want to leave? Do you want to go outside? The signs were right, but the question seemed incomprehensible to individuals who only knew the center, their only sky being the high ceiling above them.

She related her various attempts at communication when she submitted her reports, at a park, or a bar, or even a city bus stop.

Finally transferred to the clinic, Wills assisted the phlebotomist extract tissue and blood samples, cleaned up after egg donations, led inmates back to their bed in the dormitory and saw that their medications were taken. She was not required to assist with sperm donation, merely ensure the samples were securely stowed in the boxes containing dry ice and placed, as all samples and specimens, in the collection's cupboard. There was a door located on the back of this cupboard, but she never saw what might be on the other side. She ferried other samples, bone marrow, spinal fluid, stem cells, to their designated containers and placed them in the cupboard for collection. And she cleaned and sterilized all surfaces, equipment, examination chairs and any other part of the room touched by human hand or bodily fluid.

Then one shift the clinician signed: Collect One-One-Two for pre-op. Wills nodded assent and found One-One-Two in his bed. She helped him rise, waited as he went to the ablutions room to wash, and handed him his gown when he returned. Wills led him to the clinic and the clinician, who Wills knew as Attendant Thirteen, had him sit in an examination chair. She checked One-One-Two's vitals, asked him a few questions, and directed Wills to take him into the operating theater. She looked at the clinician and indicated to herself. Me? The clinician nodded, so Wills joined One-One-Two. As they neared the door, he sought her hand and gripped it.

The room looked similar to any operating theater found in any hospital. In the center was a bed. Mounted above was a powerful light, and beside it were various monitors. Wills led One-One-Two to the bed and the waiting nurse and anesthesiologist helped him lie flat. The nurse gestured to Wills to wash her hands and put gloves on. She nodded and made her way to an adjoining room. By the time she returned One-One-Two was unconscious and his bare chest was painted with betadine. His entire torso was covered in the yellow liquid. The nurse caught Wills' attention and motioned her close. The surgeon started to issue orders, not with hands, which were busy, but vocally. He asked for a scalpel, a clamp, a saw, a spreader. The names were lost to Wills. Although hearing speech in the center for the first time it was as if she were deaf.

She watched, paralyzed, as One-One-Two's heart was removed from his chest and placed carefully in a waiting cool box. An attendant rushed it away. Another attendant took his place, received two kidneys, and left. Another attendant left with two healthy lungs. Wills felt the room begin to spin and was pulled to a chair before she fell. A garbage pail seemed to miraculously appear before her and she vomited into it. She lifted watery eyes and glanced at the bed as One-One-Two continued to be dismembered, but closed them again and tears escaped. She had seen death before, it was sometimes part her job. But she had never seen such a cold and clinical murder.

After an eternity, Wills felt a hand take her arm and help her stand. The room was empty of surgeons and nurses and attendants. The only occupants were Wills, the nurse guiding her, and the remains of One-One-Two. In the clinic she was offered a pill in a small paper cup and another containing water. She recognized the sedatives that inmates were given after a procedure. Wills placed it in her mouth and swallowed, let herself be guided to a small couch beside the clinician's desk, and lay down.

You wanted to see me, Sir?

Yes, I want her moved again.

Again? She has seen, in detail, almost every aspect of the center. She just watched One-One-Two be dissected.

She will understand what she saw. Believe it or not, I know what I'm doing.

Of course, Sir.

I want her placed as a personal care assistant to Number Seventeen. Effective immediately.

You're joking! I mean ... Sir?

I'm serious. They went to the trouble of inserting her with us, and she has worked very diligently. For them and for us. Let her do her job. I think it is time she and Seventeen met. She has reports to make.

Yes, Sir.

As instructed, Wills knocked on the door before entering. A young man, brown hair, pale skin, athletic build, stood in the middle of the entry and indicated with a hand to a comfortable looking chair.

"Please, have a seat," he said. "Yes, I can speak," he added when Wills didn't move. "Come, sit."

Wills sat. She stared at the young man as he took a seat across from her.

"Thank you for coming. I've heard a lot of good things about you."

"I haven't heard anything about you," Wills said.

"Obviously," he said with a short laugh. "Your expression is priceless. But they should not have been so cruel."

"I think that is part of their nature."

"And I've heard of your experience," he said. "I'm sorry you saw that. That was cruel."

"I got off lightly," Wills said.

They stared at each other for several moments, eyes locked. Wills broke the silence. "I don't really know why I'm here."

"I think you should by now," he said. "But never mind. Maybe just to converse? I don't have many people to talk with. My world is rather small. So let's talk. You must have a hundred questions. Let's start with a few. Go on, it's okay."

"Who are you?" Wills asked.

"I'm Seventeen."

"No, I mean, who? What is your name?"

"I am Number Seventeen. It is my name, no different than any other."

"Are you the original? Are the others from you?"

He shook his head and laughed. "Goodness, no. The Original. I am the same as my brothers and sisters."

"No, you're not."

"Yes, I am," Seventeen insisted. "I can speak. I can read and learn. I can improve myself. The others could as well, but they aren't given the opportunity. It isn't necessary in their role."

"Body parts and—"

"They serve a need. If they were taught, they could do what I do. Their minds are designed for learning. They just haven't been offered the same opportunity as I." Seventeen stood. "I'm afraid I've been remiss as a host. Would you care for a drink? I have coffee and tea. Or beer. And wine. There's a very nice white in the fridge."

Wills clenched her jaw, muscles tensing visibly. "The white sounds nice, thank you," she managed to say.

He returned with two glasses, handing one to her and sitting with the other. They sipped at the same time.

"Nice place," Wills said. And it was. Modern kitchen, large living area, comfortable chairs, a hallway leading to what must be bedroom, bathroom, and a third door, open, that revealed a home office. "How long have you lived here?"

"Thank you. It is very comfortable," he answered. "And three years."

"And before then?"

"No before. Just here."

Wills drank more wine. "What does that mean?" she asked.

"Just here," he said, and then nodded. "Of course! You haven't seen the accelerant room. It would make sense if you had."

"But I haven't seen it."

"No. Maybe at a later time," Seventeen said. "It's very impressive. Each fully formed and matured at the end of the process. You have seen the results."

"I have?"

"My brothers and sisters with whom you have been working." Seventeen smiled. "This is pleasant. Conversation and wine. I'm going to enjoy our visits. My days are so routine. Fitness, study, training, more study. More training. Tell me, what is the weather like outside?"

"Rainy. Grey, at least when I arrived," Wills said. "Typical this time of year."

"Sounds wonderful. And no, I haven't been 'outside', to pre-empt your next question. Like I said, mine is very small world. Do you want to see a trick? They just taught me this. I think it's something they want you to see."

Without waiting for a reply, he rose and went into the study down the hall, coming back carrying a handgun. Wills gripped her wine glass, but Seventeen just laughed.

"Relax," he said. He opened the chamber and showed her it was empty. He went to the coffee table and knelt beside it, placing the gun in front of himself.

"9-millimeter, Glock 34 Long Slide, but you probably recognize it. Very accurate." He shook his hands and wiggled his fingers. "You don't wear a watch, so you'll have to count. Maybe I can beat my record. Ready? Just start counting when I start."

Wills watched as he quickly field-stripped and re-assembled the handgun.

"Well?" he asked.

"I forgot to count," Wills said. "A few seconds."

"The Thirty-Four is rather easy to strip, but that's part of its appeal. Do you shoot?" he asked.

Wills momentarily forgot she was Ronda. It was a charade Seventeen seemed to have dispensed with as soon as she sat. "No."

"Of course not." His smile told her he knew differently. "I'm going to enjoy our visits. I do hope you will be able to return. Would you like another wine?" He waited for her empty glass with outstretched hand, knowing her answer.

"Might as well," she said.

Agent Wills headed to her briefing. Different park. Different bench. Trees were in bud, but she pulled her coat tight in an attempt to keep out an icy wind. She saw the designated bench ahead, and who sat at it. She stopped walking for a moment, snorted, and carried on. She wasn't entirely surprised.

"Agent Wills, it's good to see you again," the woman said.

"Ma'am," Wills answered. She didn't bother to scan the area for any unwelcome observers. If this person were meeting her in the open, the time for subterfuge, for whatever reason, was at an end. Wills sat.

"I want to congratulate you on all your work," Bureau Chief Mandy Wright said. "Your reports have been invaluable. And appreciated by many who work well above our pay grade."

Wills waited.

"I'm here to take you in," Wright said. "Time to come home."

"Just like that?"

"Just like that. Job well done. We're passing the baton to another agency."

"I thought we were the ones charged with bringing killers to justice."

"It doesn't always work that way," Wright said. "The government isn't always consistent about who it works with."

"Works with?" Wills asked. "They're farming humans in there. I watched them slaughter a man. Literally take him to pieces."

"Your report was quite graphic. And all of your reports have been appreciated. But like I said, this is no longer our concern. BHS is now, for all intents and purposes, a defense contractor."

"Defense?"

"As in Department of Defense," Wright said. "Defense Intelligence Agency, to be precise."

"DIA? The ones who impersonate FBI agents and torture Jihadis? You've got to be kidding."

"The case is closed. You've done an impeccable job, and a commendation is waiting." She held up a hand before Wills could interrupt. "I've personally come to take you in because you deserve to hear it from me. And Agent Wills, just as BHS had a non-disclosure clause, the DIA has one too. Only magnitudes stricter. Do you understand?"

"Yes, Ma'am."

Wright stood. "Good. Now let's get out of this dreary park and get back to the office. There's a bit of a 'welcome back' thing arranged for you."

THE EPISTLE OF PETRIT

P etrit opened his eyes to a dark room. He pulled back the covers of his small bed and put his feet on the cold stone floor. He walked to the washbasin and splashed frigid water on his face. He ran his wet hands over his hair that stuck up unevenly despite the water. It was vain to be concerned. Slipping into his plain tunic, he rubbed his arms for warmth. Not waiting for the bells, he made his way to the chapel. Others were there before him, kneeling on the hard floor. Morning vigil, the time before the dawning of the sun, before the dawning of God's light, dispelling the darkness of ignorance, malice, and sin.

"O Lord, open thou my lips; and my mouth shall shew forth thy praise. For thou desirest not sacrifice; else would I give it: thou delightest not in burnt offering. The sacrifices of God are a broken spirit: a broken and a contrite heart, O God, thou wilt not despise."

Petrit mumbled the words quietly. He heard similar mumbling among the pews. His mind grew numb as he murmured the psalms. At the bells, he followed the others to the dining hall where a bowl of hot tea and a piece of bread awaited him. Before long, bells rang again.

Lauds, the second service of the day. Carved in the stone of the lintel of the chapel entrance was a promise: *sepientian sapientum perdam*. I will destroy the wisdom of the wise. Paul, championing faith. "Praise God, the Creator of Light! Praise Christ, the Son of God, who has risen, Victor over Satan, sin, and death!" Darkness vanquished. A new day begun. Yet another day.

Petrit made his way back to his cell for *lectio devina*, the divine reading. An hour to listen for the word of God through study of his written Word. *Lectio, meditatio, oratio, contemplatio*. Read, meditate, pray, contemplate. Petrit closed his door and sat at the small table that was his desk. He opened the one and only book in the room. There was a crease running down the spine that made this selection inevitable. Paul's epistle. An open letter. Like all letters. No privacy existed, not even within his mind.

"Watch out for those that create dissension," Paul warns.

"Professing to be wise, they became fools and exchanged the glory of the incorruptible God for an image in the form of corruptible man and of birds and four-footed animals and crawling creatures. Therefore, God gave them over in the lusts of their hearts to impurity, so that their bodies would be dishonored among them. For they exchanged the truth of God for a lie and worshiped and served the creature rather than the Creator, who is blessed forever. Amen."

Petrit thought of the women in the nearby village. An entire village of women, dressed in plain habits, heads covered, away from any temptations of the flesh, listening for the word of God. And waiting for the bells to announce *Terce*, the third mass of the day, followed by hours of work in the fields or factories. It was their fate, just as it was his own. Born second, or third, or fourth, or fifth. Only the eldest can take a surname, carry on the family line, and become parishioners. The first son and the first daughter. All others are destined to serve

God through serving the church and the state. Some found to have the right aptitude were made Guardians, policing action and thought. The universe had an order, and that order was divine. Augustine of Hippo had made that clear.

Petrit opened his book randomly again and read: "Make no provision for the flesh to fulfil lusts thereof." Paul's letters again. Love for Christ is enough. At least for second or third or fourth or fifth born. Let them show their love through labor.

But Petrit no longer loved Christ. He started writing his own letter, trying to describe the worlds he had seen. He knew there were many other worlds, some vastly different from his. His knowledge made the stones beneath his knees harder, the morning chill more penetrating, the words he spoke and read emptier. He hid the sheaths of paper inside his old mattress. It was a sign of weakness, or of strength—Petrit didn't know which—that he hoped others would one day see it. If he were alive when it was found he would be burnt as a heretic. A release from this life, at least. Petrit knew it was sin to think that. He smiled inwardly.

Paul warned against unbelief and the wrath of God. It wasn't that Petrit didn't entirely believe—he knew there was a something out there. It was that he no longer believed the words. The Word. He had seen too much, and he didn't trust them. Or the god those words spoke of. There were too many gods, each with their own agenda, to be trusted. Angles, daemons, gods, whatever they wished to be called.

Petrit dreamed he saw Paul of Tarsus. He stood by a stone wall, eyes wide at the vivid scene passing in front of him. People passed by him, men *and* women, even children! They wore light gowns, tied at the shoulder or gathered at the waist with a colorful belt. Their hair flowed behind them. Petrit joined the crowd. He could feel a wide grin stretching his face. It was so bright. So warm. So real. He looked at his bare arms and followed them down to his hands. That was when he knew he was dreaming. That was the thought that woke him: *I am dreaming!*

Vigils. Hot tea. Lauds. *Lectio devina*. Work. The next day he couldn't concentrate on the world around him. Vespers. Supper. Compline, the final service of the day. "Lord, let your servant depart in peace." Mouthing the words that the others sang. And finally, lights out.

Petrit slept and dreamed and returned to the busy scene. He looked at his hands, knowing he was dreaming or something else entirely, but managed to hold on this time. He contained his excitement and stayed. He smiled and lifted his face to the sun. He watched the people moving around, and he thought about the freedom of their movement. The uninhibited laughter of women played in his ears. He walked along the wall, following the crowd. He passed tables along the way and merchants selling everything, from sandals to dried fish to small statues. Petrit looked at a statuette, a small figurine that had no resemblance to Mary. There was no modesty in this figure. She stood proudly, one breast bared. Petrit looked away, blushing at the sight of her erect nipple.

Ahead stood the frontage of the amphitheater. The people were filing inside the enclosure and filling the rows of stone seats surrounding the arena. Petrit watched from a distance, too timid to enter. He did not belong, and yet he knew somehow that he was there for a purpose. His ignorance was soon dispelled.

On the third night, the archangel Michael appeared. He stood before Petrit and extended his glorious wings. "You are here to protect my prophet," he said. "Ensure it is done. Remember and return." Petrit immediately woke, gasping in his lonely cell. The archangel's voice still echoed in his mind. Michael, the leader of all angels and of the army of God against the rebel Lucifer and his horde, defender of heaven, leading all believers in battle against heresy.

That was when Petrit still believed in stories of archangels and divine guidance. Before he knew what Michael really was.

On the fourth night, Petrit saw Paul of Tarsus. Paul the apostle, Paul the evangelist, without whom the Church would be nothing but a fringe sect, as it is on other worlds. But Paul spread the Word, and Christ's message took root, growing into the mighty tree that offered shade to all mankind. The Book of Acts tells the story: Paul, a Pharisee participating in the persecution of the disciples of Jesus until he was blinded by a terrific light, fell to the ground and was lifted by the resurrected Jesus. Paul was reformed, reborn, and baptized in the new faith, proclaiming Jesus as the Messiah, the Son of God.

Paul was arguing with a stallholder. Paul picked up a statuette of the beautiful woman with the bare breast and smashed it on the stone path. Then he stormed off towards the theatre. Petrit struggled to keep up. Stallholders shouted at Paul, and some spat, but he continued righteously marching forward. Paul turned down a narrow lane. As Petrit turned the corner, he stumbled into the back of a man and accidently pushed him against a wall. There was a clatter as a knife dropped from the man's hand and onto the ground. Petrit stooped and grasped the blade, understanding as he picked it up that the other intended to kill Paul and that he was there to stop him. He did not know from where this knowledge sprang, only a certainty as to why he was at this place and time. To protect the prophet, the one so instrumental in shaping Petrit's world. The man's eyes filled with surprise and he gasped as Petrit pushed the knife into his abdomen. He pulled the blade out and stabbed again. Blood stained the wall behind as he slid to the ground. Petrit dropped the bloodied knife and watched as the would-be assassin died.

Petrit woke in his cell, screaming. He stuck his hand in his mouth to stop the noise lest he wake another. Petrit lay in his single bed throughout the remaining dark hours, feeling his heart beat rapidly in his chest.

Vigils. Hot tea. *Lauds. Lectio devina*. Work. *Vespers*. Supper. *Compline*. "Lord, let your servant depart in peace. Please, God, protect me this night."

And finally, lights out.

Michael was standing beside Petrit when he opened his eyes. The archangel touched his arm, sending a jolt of electricity throughout his entire body. Petrit knew on a level so deep and dark he could not see, that it wasn't Michael beside him, but something else. Words echoed in his mind.

"My son, our defender," Michael said. He handed Petrit a cloth bundle. "Take this and slay the heretic, Pelagius." The creature's wings extended to their full glory. He pointed a sword forward, down the small hill on which they stood, to a provincial city surrounded by a stone wall.

Petrit unwrapped the cloth parcel and held a knife in his hand.

"You will defend the faith. Come. I will guide you," Michael said as he strode down the hill.

Petrit followed. They entered the gates of the city unhindered, down winding lanes and past numerous villas. Michael stopped at an opened doorway, which led to an inner courtyard. Petrit stepped through. Pelagius was easy to find. A young man sat alone at a table in the courtyard. He stood as Petrit approached, but he noticed the knife too late. Petrit acted as if the hand of Michael guided his. He stabbed Pelagius in his stomach and sliced sideways before withdrawing the blade. Pelagius grimaced in agony, clutched his stomach, and fell to his knees.

He held his wound and gazed at Petrit. "Why?" the young man gasped.

"You are the heretic, Pelagius. I am defending the faith," Petrit stammered.

"Please, help me," he was answered.

Petrit dropped the knife and knelt beside the young man. He put a hand on his shoulder. "I am doing Michael's bidding," Petrit said. I follow Michael's bidding."

"You have done this. None made you." Pelagius' voice was hoarse. He tried to push Petrit away but his strength ebbed with his blood. Petrit sat and took the man's head in his lap.

"Lie still," Petrit said lamely. "It is God's will. It is ordained to pass."

"You kill me. You did this. It is you and only you that chooses your action. You choose to sin." Pelagius coughed, and blood trickled from his mouth.

Petrit thought about the heresy as Pelagius' body grew lifeless. Humans cannot choose freely. That was part of God's great plan. And men could not avoid sinning as if it were a matter of choosing. They were born in sin, forever tainted by the shame and guilt of the Original Sin. That was what Petrit was taught. That was why all were baptized as infants, to cleanse from that sin. If men could avoid sin, they would be free … No. There was no freedom. There was only God's will. And he was doing God's will. Michael had led him to this place to do God's will, the guide behind all of our actions. If the will of man is free, then there need be no church. There need be no God.

Petrit gently set the dead man's head on the courtyard floor and stood. He backed away and stared at the corpse. Then he turned and ran out of the courtyard and blindly through twisting streets. Finally, he stumbled into an alley. He collapsed against a wall with his bloodied hands to his face. Red painted his cheeks.

"Despair not, Petrit," Michael said. "You have been chosen by me to do great things. You will wake now and reflect on what you have achieved. The heretic Pelagius is no more. He will never be. His heresy will not infect the flock. It lies stillborn on the stones beside his corpse. Sing your praise to God. Delight in your worship."

Michael touched Petrit on the head, and the jolt woke him. He lay in his darkened cell, waiting for the light of dawn. As day approached, he rose and went through the routine, numb to his surroundings. And then he learned to dream and travel on his own.

Grace to you and peace from your own inner place of worship, Petrit wrote on stolen stationary, mocking the letters of Paul to the emergent Christian community in Corinth. Paul continued after his greeting about the benefits of the ongoing suffering with which the community was afflicted. As Petrit wrote he felt both liberated, yet also stained. The culture of his birth was ingrained too deeply as was adherence to the one true faith. Reward and punishment, carrot and stick, used with children and animals alike. He glanced over his shoulder as he wrote but there was no pounding on the door or punishment from above and he continued writing in the candle light to his community of one.

I have been groomed, this paper read, discovered under his bunk during a surprise inspection and taken away by a monk ordered to destroy it in the purifying flames with its author. *But I was groomed my whole life. All there is is the faith, and that's all I knew. It's hard to think outside the box when you don't even know you're in one. And it's even harder when you see what happens when people do. Terrible things. I was taught there is only one God. There was nothing more. There was no alternative. All-seeing, all-knowing, all-powerful. Talk about control! Even inside your mind, there is no privacy. A god that sees all can see your thoughts, your doubts, your fears. I grew up with our stories, the ones parents and priests tell, so I was a faithful, fearful soldier.*

And when the archangel came to me ... me! ... I felt chosen. Special. I did what it wanted. I am not making excuses. I have sinned greatly and my soul may never be clean. Most people don't even remember what they have done in their dreams. I remembered, and I kept doing it. But there was that moment on the mountain, surrounded by desert when I stood and saw the blood on my hands. Real blood. And I had no idea why. I just did what I was instructed to do. Follow the Arab into the cave in mountain known as Hira by the city of Mecca and bash out his life as he prays.

I have been transformed from mere monk to mindless killer and told to be glad that I do the Lord's work. How can that be? I dream and I am transported to different times. To different worlds. Yes, they exist! I was taught there was but one God. And yet I have found there is a whole pantheon of gods. Give them wings and call them angels. Give them horns and call them devils. They're all part of the story. But when you start pulling on strings, like the loose thread on your tunic that begins to unravel ... It was terrifying. A whole life of being trained not to think or doubt, story after story of faithful obedience and unimaginable punishment. Stop your doubting and believe! The greatest thinkers have said so. The disease of curiosity. 'It is this that drives us to try and discover the secrets of nature, those secrets which are beyond our understanding, which can avail us nothing and which man should not wish to learn.' That is Augustine himself.

But I failed at faith. Instead of trying to guard my mind, I opened it. I asked a simple question: why does an angel want me to kill? What is it afraid of? If it has fear, is it weak? If it needs me, does that mean I have strength? If it cannot do it itself, is not that a weakness? I started sleeping with these questions. I tried to focus my intention, tried to narrow my focus. I wanted to understand.

Remember, dear sceptic, blessed thinker, to remember your dreaming. Make that an intention as you lay your head down. Clear your mind of all expectations, enter the emptiness open and aware. Notice when you are dreaming and participate. Acknowledge you are dreaming, explore the world where you may find yourself. See that there are many ways.

I dreamed and found myself in a library. I did not even know what a library was until I opened my eyes in my dreaming and saw one. Imagine books and scrolls everywhere! Not copies of the One Book, but all different types full of thoughts and histories and ancient learnings. At first, I spent most of the time looking over my shoulder, but there was nothing or nobody to stop me and I got lost among the shelves. I avoided Michael and his biddings and came back to the library every night, but not just to that library but others as well, and I spent every lectio devina reading in these other worlds. For that was what they were. Ours is not the only reality. It is but one among many. I spent my sleep trying to understand, to make sense, of what I saw and read.

I came across names in books, and also looked for ones I knew. Pelagius. Arius. Paul of Tarsus. Augustine. Epicurus. I killed Pelagius! I was given a knife and instructions in a dream, and I watched his life drain away with his blood on the courtyard stones. In my world he does not exists. There is no heresy of free will. And yet I found books about his life and his thoughts, words that he wrote long after I was there. Other worlds where he lived. I realized that I was being used to get rid of ideas before they could grow, ideas that could open minds, teaching them to question the dogmas that anchor our faith and belief. Believing is a giving of energy. The believer gives their energy to the idea, and the idea becomes real. Or the angel or daemon or god becomes manifest.

But time kills all things. Even the gods. That's why they interfere so much. They just want to live longer. It's pathetic, really. Pelagius spoke about the freedom to find our own salvation. What terrific implications! With that freedom, what use do we have for gods, one or many? Augustine ... I found worlds where he did not exist! Or maybe he did but died before his poison could flow from his quill. Man tainted and damaged from the beginning of time, trapped in a shameful, filthy body, a body to be despised because it comes between the soul and its god. Such a hateful message.

There is no Augustine in some worlds, where people celebrate their humanity. Bodies are a form of celebrating life. I think wherever Augustine poisoned a culture, people feel a little differently about themselves. Or a lot differently about themselves. I have seen in some cultures that the body is seen as a gift from God. 'I am created in the image of the gods!' They exclaim. 'Look at me, touch me. Let me touch you. Let us celebrate! Let us worship each other!'

In a culture poisoned by Augustine, the body is seen as bad, pleasuring the body as sinful, and touching another as wrong. They hate their bodies. Augustine was so disgusted by his body that he delighted in punishing it. When he died, a stream of insects was seen fleeing his cold corpse. It strikes me as disgusting now, but those around Augustine thought of him as a saint. Can one person make such a difference to a culture? Or a world? I think so. If Augustine wasn't there, would somebody else have said the same? I think not.

I have seen cusps of time when a person is removed or never becomes. I have been there during such cusps.

I ask you not to believe, but to disbelieve everything you have been told since birth. Open your mind to realities branching out at key moments. What am I saying? Different worlds? Infinite realities? Yes! And actual participation in shaping them. Decisions made in cusps creating whole new timelines, or altering a timeline. Wake in the dawn for another purpose beside prayer and work.

Like the veins under your skin, fine blue lines, branching off, going this way and that. All these veins and arteries radiating out from the source, the heart. At the point where one branches from the other, imagine that as one of these cusps. An epochal moment. I protect the evangelist Paul and a church grows. I kill the heretic Pelagius and an idea dies. I stone a prophet in a lonely cave and a future world religion is snuffed out. And Michael and his ilk grow stronger.

It is all energy. Life is energy. Instead of a heart, there is a center of this energy. Maybe that is the oneness so many gnostic and heretical traditions speak of and try to describe and name. Energy radiating outward in a web of life and realities. And what we call gods and angels and devils are energies like us, only more powerful in the realm of energy. We give them names and we give them power. The more we give, the stronger they become. When we stop giving energy, they fade. They die. Just like us.

There they are, pulling the strings. These points in time are the playground of the gods, where they use us, on our many worlds and realities and where I was used. But that need not be the case anymore.

At dawn, the outer locks of his quarters were unlocked. Two monks entered, pulled him roughly to his feet, and wrenched his arms behind his back. Pain shot through his shoulders. They bound his hands tightly. One gave a hard shove to the small of his back and Petrit stumbled towards the door, hitting the frame and causing a new streak of blood to trickle down his face. The monks didn't laugh. They showed no emotion, not even pleasure, just like in his beating the day before.

They grabbed him roughly by his tunic. He stumbled and was steadied, pushed a little less aggressively, just enough so he would stay on his feet. The monks didn't speak. Words were for those deserving empathy, or even merely acknowledgment. All Petrit deserved was death, and that was all they were going to give him.

As he entered the communal grounds, a priest waited. When Petrit neared the priest spat and turned his back. Those standing near the priest turned with him. The monks led him to the center of the grounds where a post stood on a small wooden platform. Dry scrub packed under and around the platform provided tinder. Petrit smelled the oil that it was soaked in. He walked up the small flight of steps and stood in front of the post. The monks turned him around to face the gathered crowd. All were summoned for the occasion. And all were facing away from him.

The monks bound his neck to the poll with a coarse rope. They tied his feet together at the base, and a final length around his waist. Then they descended without a word and joined the line of monks formed on the left. Petrit turned his head as far he could and surveyed the backs of his fellow community members. All had turned their backs on him.

A priest stepped forward, carrying a lit torch. He held Petrit's letter as if it were covered in excrement, brought it close to the torch until the papers began to burn. Then he unceremoniously bent to the platform and touched the flame to the oil-soaked scrub. As it caught light, he tossed in the torch and turned, walking back to his place among the others. Black smoke rose around Petrit. He coughed as it first entered his lungs, but that was the only sound he made. Soon all that could be heard was the crackle of the fire as is it devoured everything in its reach. The smell of burning meat mingled with that of wood and oil.

The priest returned to his quarters after the purification was complete, the day run its course and it was the period of *lectivo devina*. He had difficulty reconciling such ceremonies with the teachings of forgiveness and redemption found in certain scripture. Have not all sinned? How can he cast the first stone? And yet he did, with flame. He closed the door of his small cell and secured it by wedging his chair against it. The he knelt and lifted a sandstone floor tile. He withdrew the manuscript confiscated from the heretic Petrit. Perhaps he was himself a heretic, burning mere blank pages to use as torch, and retaining the forbidden words.

Grace to you and peace from your own inner place of worship, he began to read.

THE RUNNER

"That the cargo?" Curls asked.

She pointed to a short brunette wearing eye glasses, a worn wool sweater and skirt. Obviously going for the nerdy look. Maybe Skip's new kink, it wasn't for her to judge. Everyone was welcome to their own taste. It would just be nice if he didn't bring it into the hangar. Glasses. Seriously. Nobody wore glasses. Because nobody had eyes that needed glasses. Probably just part of the costume. Still, Curls had to admit, it was kind of sexy. She let her eyes travel down the woman's narrow waist and smooth, short legs. Thick, muscular calves. If she were an actual librarian or secretary or whatever, she also liked to hike.

"Yeah, that's the cargo," Skip answered.

"Do you have to bring them here?" Curls asked. "Can't you just leave them in bed?"

"Jealous?"

"You wish."

"You have no idea," Skip said, pinching her bottom. Curls hit his hand away and clenched a fist, ready to use it.

"But I'm serious," Skip said. "Let me introduce you to our 'cargo', seeing as that's your department." He walked over to the woman waiting at the entrance of the camouflaged hangar followed by Curls.

"First Mate Curls," Skip said formally, "I'd like to introduce our most valuable passenger on the *Cricket*, Astrogator Sarah Christine, who has an appointment with a starship currently waiting near the planet Mercury."

"Shit," Curls stammered, wiping her hand on her jumpsuit before giving it to the other woman. "Pleased to meet you! An astrogator! I've never met one. Ms. ... Doctor ... Christine."

Skip put a hand on Curls' shoulder and gave a brief shake. "And now you have," he said. "See that she is very comfortable."

"I will. Shit," Curls said again, staring at the woman. "I thought you were ... never mind, follow me." She picked up the astrogator's small bag and guided her guest toward the *Cricket*.

"Call me Sarah," she said. "Is that your real name, Curls?"

"No, no, no," Curls answered. "It's because of the hair." She rubbed a palm over her shaved head. "It used to be Three-C, cause well, of what I do. Comms, cargo and ..." Curls quickly indicated her groin area.

"Seriously?" Sarah asked.

"No, I'm sorry," Curls said. "Just a bad joke. Working with guys out here tends to do that to you. Crass. Sorry. No, Comms, cargo and computers. Three-C. My name changed when I cut my hair. Much easier out here. It just turns into a mess of tangles ..." Curls trailed off as she realized she was rambling.

"Are you the only woman?" Sarah asked.

"Yeah," Curls answered. "There's Skip, who you met. I thought you were ... never mind. And Ritty. He handles anything that can kill you. Well, kill anything besides you, or us. Weapons systems. And he's the mechanic. He keeps us running, and running fast. Best kind of security, if you ask me, running fast away from danger. I don't know how he got his name. Don't know if I want to. And Charles. Our pilot. That's his real name, I think." She stopped, rambling again.

"Small crew," Sarah said.

"It's better that way."

Sarah waited for more, but the woman beside her was, for the first time, quiet. She followed her gaze to the ship. Curls smiled proudly but the astrogator felt a degree of anxiety at having volunteered for the mission. Command made it abundantly clear that she could get killed doing it. But even if they assured her the *Cricket* was her best chance, the look of the ship didn't instill confidence.

"Don't let appearances fool you," Curls said, noticing her guest's expression. "She's the fastest runner there is, our little *Cricket*."

Cricket looked as well used as she was. Burns scarred a once a glistening silver hull. Most marking were from re-entry, but others definitely from more hostile origins. She was still sleek, Sarah admitted. A narrow cone widened into a cylindrical mid-section, ending with stubby fins and a very large reactor and propulsion system. It was clear where her speed came from.

"Come inside, I'll show you where you'll be bunking," Curls said.

They climbed a ladder and entered a hatch, emerging into a wide empty area. "This is my office," Curls said, waving a hand over the cargo room. "One of them, anyway. Come this way." She strode off to a forward hatch, ducked through it and stopped.

"Here are the sleepers," she said, indicating six cryo-pods as she passed. "I'll prep one for you as soon as we're ready."

Curls walked forward again and stopped at another hatch. She opened it to reveal a small cabin, large enough for a bunk, the astrogator's small bag, and little else.

"Sanitation is that hatch there." Curls pointed across the corridor. "Well," she said, when her guest didn't move. "Make yourself comfortable, have a rest, and I'll see you in a short while."

She pointed to the cabin and shrugged and Sarah understood she wanted her out of the way. Ducking her head, she entered, sat on the bunk and the woman with the shaved head disappeared. Sarah sat on the bunk and listened through the bulkhead. A hatch opened and slammed shut.

Curls headed straight to the mess where she found Skip, Ritty and Charles.

"What the fuck are you playing at?" Curls demanded. The internal bulkheads were surprisingly thin, and their guest listened to the conversation.

"Making money. Keeping us flying. Doing my job," Skip answered.

"Don't be a smart ass!" Curls called. "An astrogator? A starship? You've lost your fucking mind!"

"The money's good," the captain said.

"Not if we're dead and can't spend it!"

"We're not going to die," Skip retorted. "We're going to make a lot of dough and be able to take that break you've been wanting."

"And buy the new tech you wanted for your computers.".

"Shut up, Charles!"

"You might throw our lives away, but an astrogator's too valuable," Curls shouted.

"There's no point of having an astrogator if you don't have a starship," Skip said. "I'm just putting the two together."

"And making a huge commission."

"Shut up, Charles!" Glass broke. Sarah imagined the shaved headed young woman throwing a mug or plate.

"Why doesn't the starship have its own astrogator?" Curls asked.

"I don't know. Died, probably. Calm down and listen," Skip said.

"Don't you dare tell me to calm down!"

"Okay, okay," Skip said. The smart tone had left and he sounded almost sincere. "I know this looks like suicide, but hear us out—"

"Us?"

"Us. The crew—"

"You three and your dumb cocks—"

"Fuck me," Skip groaned. "Ritty, tie her up and gag her so she'll at least listen.'

"Not doing that, boss," Ritty said. Sarah liked Ritty's voice, or maybe the conviction in it.

"Fine," Skip said, even more conciliation in his tone. "I am going to sit back down now and place my hands on the table. And then I am going to talk. All I ask is for you to listen. Just give me a few minutes."

It was quiet for a moment. Sarah visualized Curls sitting down. Maybe giving her captain a curt nod. Or a grimace.

"We've been offered a choice job, and I'm sorry I didn't come straight to you to hash it out. They caught me by surprise and needed an answer prompt like," Skip started. Sarah shook her head in the other room and wondered if Curls was shaking hers at the same time.

"I'm sorry, that sounded like an excuse, and if I'm honest it kind of is." Sarah was disappointed at the man's inability to dig himself out of his own hole. "They didn't just come with an offer, they came with a plan."

"A good plan," Ritty added.

"That's okay, Ritty," Skip said. "Let me."

"Sure, boss."

"The contract is to escort astrogator Sarah Christine, who is no doubt listening to all this because the internal bulkheads are so damn thin—Hi Sarah—to a waiting ship beyond the blockade. It's been waiting near the sun for months. When she gets her astrogator, we'll follow in the *Cricket* and get back home."

"There and back, in and out, money in the bank."

"Shut up, Charles!" Curls and Skip shouted at the same time.

"Out to the ship. Come back home," Curls said.

"That's right," Skip said, obviously missing something in the way Curls said it, at least how Sarah heard it.

"We won't even get out of the atmosphere before the plasma canon on those fucking alien platforms vaporizes us," Curls said.

"That's what I said to Command," Skip confessed. "Suicide. Might as well shoot ourselves in the head and do it quicker."

"He said that," Ritty agreed.

"But then they showed me the plan of how we're going to break the blockade," Skip said. "The plan you're going to improve and make work."

"It's a good plan," Ritty agreed. "You need to see it."

"What he said," Skip said. "At least look at it. It's crazy. It's ballsy. It's original. I think you're going to like it."

Silence followed. Sarah imagined Ritty smiling and nodding. Charles waiting quietly. Skip timidly hoping.

"Fine," Curls finally said. "Let me see their damn plan."

A hand slapped the table. "Excellent! Boys, take our very brilliant computer technician and show her the play."

Curls knocked on Sarah's hatch before putting her head into the small space. "I'm going to be tied up for a while analyzing the flight plan," she said. "There's coffee and tea in the mess. Help yourself to any chow. Really, make yourself at home." And then she disappeared.

Four hours later, Curls was back. She found Sarah sitting motionless at the mess table, staring at a spot on the wall. Curls watched from the hatchway for a moment before entering.

"You okay?" she asked.

"Yes, thank you. I was just reading," Sarah said.

Curls glanced around for a tablet or book, but then laughed and tapped her face. "The glasses! Of course. I thought they were just an accessory. You look cute with them. I mean, you look cute without them, but—"

"I understand," Sarah said.

"I've heard about them," Curls said.

"Do you want a try," Sarah asked.

"Yes. But no. Not right now, anyway. There's still lots to do." After all the modifications and preparations, there really wasn't much left. But it was time to secure the 'cargo'.

"Sorry," Sarah said. "Do you need the mess? Should I go back to my quarters?"

"Your closet, you mean," Curls laughed. "No. I need you. You need to strip down to your undies and stow your gear. Then come with me."

"Strip here?"

"No, you can strip in your quarters if you want."

"Okay," Sarah said without moving.

"Seriously," Curls said, starting to remove her own boots and pants. "But there's more space here. I always hit my head in my box."

Sarah left the mess, crawled into her quarters and removed her clothes, hitting her head on a bulkhead in the process. She packed her clothes away and put her bag in the one drawer under the bunk. When she came out, Curls was waiting, wearing her undies, a sports bra and a smile.

"Cute," she said. Then: "Come with me, your pod is ready."

Curls led the astrogator to an open cryo-pod. Sarah had seen many but never used one. She carefully touched it, as if it were a hungry animal wanting to eat her.

Curls placed a hand on her shoulder. "It's okay, you just climb in and lie down," she said.

"That's what I'm afraid of."

"Really, it's okay." Curls guided the astrogator into the pod. She felt her reluctance, but Sarah sat when prompted. She lifted each leg and nestled into the gel.

"This part of the plan isn't my favorite, but it's pretty essential," Curls said. "We all have to go in."

Sarah moved her head, looking at the gel surrounding her. "I don't want to die in one of these," she confessed.

"Not going to happen," Curls said. "I was skeptical at first, you probably heard. But it's a good plan. And if we do die, we'll never even know it. Not that we're going to!" she added when Sarah's eyes widened.

"We're going to miss all the fun, and then wake up by your star-ship," Curls said. "You'll feel a prick, and bit sleepy, and then we'll be at the starship. Okay?'

"Okay," Sarah said, feeling a prick below her ribs. Curls stood above her smiling.

"You're really cute," she heard Curls say. And then she didn't hear or see anything.

Curls moved to her own cryo-pod once ground crew moved the ship to the launch pad. She lay back, winced when the needle pierced her and injected the chemicals into her liver needed to induce the coma-like hyperthermia. She ran through her programming again, futilely fighting the coming sleep. It was too late to do anything differently. No way to tweak, improve, change. Abort. She did all there was to do. So she closed her eyes and slept.

The ship was tilted to ninety degrees for lift off. As the crew inside slumbered, ancillary fuel cylinders were attached to its body. This was no gradual ascent into the stratosphere, no comfortable time-consuming climb, higher and higher, to escape the planet's gravity. They had no time to dally. The plan to break the blockade was based on speed. And unpredictability. And deception. Curls liked what Command had offered, but it had weaknesses to replace with strengths, or at least creative maneuvers to give them a fighting chance. Skip asked what she thought the odds were. She lied and told him seventy-thirty. She wished it were as high as fifty-fifty.

Orbiting above the planet were three massive alien platforms, bristling with plasma canon and very alert detection systems. That was the *Crickets* first chance. There were only three, which meant at the vague place where atmosphere turned into space, there had to be a blind spot. Not a big one, but a spot nonetheless. The nerds at Command did well to find it. Outside of that very small blind spot there was a large field of debris. As soon as the aliens arrived, they promptly blasted every ship and satellite orbiting the planet to smithereens. That was chance number two. Lots of debris meant lots of cover. But debris didn't fly on a course away from the planet. Only blockade runners did that, and the guns on the platforms could tell the difference. That's where chance number three increased their odds.

The *Cricket* launched and increased speed as it fought to free itself from the planet's grip. It shot upward, each second increasing the distance from the launch site, increasing the velocity and gravities experienced on board. In each cryo-pod, gel filled any space, cushioning those within. At thirty-five thousand meters, the first ring of danger began. The ship expelled two decoys that continued upwards while *Cricket* arched to the left, angling for the blind spot. One decoy was hit almost instantaneously. The second decoy lasted fourteen seconds, four more than Curls predicted. Meanwhile, the force within the accelerating ship reached fifteen gravities, then sixteen.

Then *Cricket* left the atmosphere and into the emptiness of space. Only it wasn't empty. The course Curls was given provided safe passage through the debris field. Safe from the debris, anyway. As they passed through, the closest potential threat from debris was two kilometers away. Curls changed that, bringing it nearer to two hundred meters. She would never know if her calculations were incorrect. Four more decoys launched in close succession as it passed, and *Cricket* lurched again. The force of the movement would have reduced any biological matter, like a person, to a smudge of red goo. But all such matter was safely contained in a gel-filled cryo-pod. The decoys joined the orbiting debris in four rapid explosions, three from plasma bursts and the fourth by the debris itself.

But the *Cricket* continued. Clear of the debris field she released twelve decoys and veered to starboard. Then the computer controlling *Cricket* initiated Curls' main addition to the plan. Additional decoys were an advantage. She asked for three times more than originally suggested and got them. When she installed those, she asked for something she didn't even know they had, the only thing that brought the odds somewhere closer to even. Command provided them, and Ritty took pleasure in mounting the weapons on the ship. As the *Cricket* veered, it attacked the nearest platform. First a salvo of missiles accelerated away from the ship. *Cricket* veered to port and fired another salvo. Each missile shot forward at incredible force, then the multiple warheads within each missile spread out and sped towards their target.

Cricket zigged and zagged as the missiles exploded, a display of fireworks without sound, and without audience. The crew of the *Cricket,* and their one passenger, grew farther away from the blockade and closer to safety. Behind them a cannon locked onto the solitary flare trying to escape. It fired and a warhead, following its own mad goal of destruction, strayed into the path, just at the right time, and exploded into thousands of pieces of debris. In a millisecond, the cannon on the alien platform readjusted aim but overheated and could fire no more.

Just as programmed, halfway to the starship the *Cricket* ceased accelerating. Inside, the tremendous force that pressed on the ship eased. But none inside felt it. They continued to sleep. Thrusters tilted the ship to vertical and brought it back to the horizontal. And then the massive reactors fired again as the ship began its long deceleration.

Curls blinked into the light as the lid of her cryo-pod opened and folded back into its shelf under the bed. She carefully flexed her fingers and toes, tentatively shifted her arms and legs. Moved her head left and right, checking everything still worked. Her private fear was not the cryo-pod malfunctioning—that would be a mercifully quick way to go. Her pre-sleep sweats and palpitations came from worry about the gel. If one area failed, whatever body part there would be turned into a gelatinous mess, only discovered upon revival. Curls swallowed and lifted her neck, confirming everything worked. Then she worried about the others.

She climbed out of her pod to see Skip, Ritty and Charles emerge from theirs, arms and legs full of flesh, fluid and bone. She leaned over and looked into the astrogator's pod. Misty brown eyes stared back.

Curls broke away from their grip and checked the rest of her body. Just those cute legs and arms and belly and ...

"Are we there?" Sarah asked.

Curls moved her eyes to Sarah's.

"Surprisingly, we actually are," she said. Then a wide grin spread across her face. "Fucking A, we're alive!" she laughed. She wanted to slap a hand or a shoulder, but the others were already at their stations. She took Sarah's hand and helped her out of the cryo-pod.

"How do you feel? All good?"

"My fingers and toes are tingling," Sarah answered.

"That's a good sign," Curls said. "Perfectly normal. It'll go away soon. Hopefully. Hold onto the pod until you get used to floating. Then let's get a drink. Good to hydrate. The body needs it."

Curls started to move to the mess and stopped when she noticed Sarah still floating beside the pod in her underwear.

"Oh, clothes. Dress first, then drink. Right. Working with this lot you get used to each other in their skivvies," she said as she headed to her own quarters and slipped into a flight suit.

Sarah joined her minutes later wearing what she boarded with, a sweater that covered her neck, a skirt ending at her knees, tights and her dark framed glasses. The skirt floated about her waist and would probably not last long. Skirts in free-fall were impractical, but Sarah's appeared to have a pair of shorts sewn into the inside. Curls tried not to stare as she handed her a sachet of water. Maybe it was thinking she was going to die, and finding she was alive, was causing all the blood to rush from her brain and into her groin. Sarah placed a hand on hers as she took the water and electricity shot through Curls' body.

"Thanks," Sarah said. She opened the sachet deftly and swallowed the contents without a drop escaping.

"That wasn't your first time," Curls said, hoping they were flirting.

"No," Sarah said, locking eyes. "Do me again, please."

Curls grabbed another sachet after a synapse finally fired and she realized what the astrogator meant. As she handed a water over, Skip floated into the room.

"Ah, I thought as much," he said, smirking at Curls. "You'll have to excuse my crew member, she's needed on the bridge."

"Are we nearing the Starship?" Sarah asked.

"We should be there in two hours," Skip said. "You'll feel the docking. Then you go to work."

"Thank you, Captain," she said.

"Just 'Skip'." He floated out of the mess followed by Curls.

"And you criticize me," he said under his breath.

"She's really cute," Curls whispered.

They gazed at the collection of ships through the windows.

"Crowded here," she said. "But that looks exciting." She indicated a vessel different than the rest.

"Something new called a Dreadnought," Skip said. "A very big battleship. The astrogator is going to plot a course, and we're going to follow them back home—"

"I was wondering how we were going to get back," Curls said.

"There's quite a few guns strapped on it," Skip added.

"Nice," Ritty said.

"They want a full record of our run, so send that asap," Skip said. "They're going to use our run to plan their attack."

"I still don't know why they couldn't do their own reconnaissance," Curls said.

"Yeah, well, they are, in a way. The wanted the best, so they came to us. And we didn't just get a contract. We got drafted. That bit about 'deciding' to go was just to make you feel better about it."

"Fuck you," Curls said.

"That's 'Fuck you, sir', if you please. Show some military discipline. We're in the army now."

"Any more secrets you'd like to share with your first mate?" Curls asked.

"Not that I can remember."

"Just make sure they actually pay us." Curls turned to Skip and offered a bad example of a salute. "Sir."

Black Site

The first interrogator slammed his fist into the prisoner's head. His head jerked to the side and blood flew from his punished mouth. The interrogator struck him again, this time with his left. The man strapped to the chair lurched the other direction. More blood filled his mouth and he spat it out. Even if they asked him questions, he was determined to resist. But they asked nothing, said nothing, they'd been silent since he was led into the room and strapped to the chair with plastic ties. He stared at his interrogator, waiting for him to demand information. But he didn't. He simply shook his hand, balled it again, and struck. Pain shot through the prisoner's face. He was sure his cheek bone was broken, but he didn't have time to dwell on it. The interrogator's fist slammed into the other side of his face, fracturing bones on that side, and with barely a pause stuck again. Left, right, left right.

The man in the chair tried to focus on who was hitting him. There was a pause in the torture when his interrogator shook both hands and spoke to the person next to him. He didn't know much of the language but recognized the tongue of the invader, the *zindiq*. He tried to focus his blurred eyes on the men punishing him, but they looked similar. He stared at the one with bruised fists and then at his companion, and he saw the same person. He didn't have time to reflect on what he saw, as he was hit again, and again, and again, until everything became dark. After he lost consciousness, the beating continued, only ending when both of his interrogators were certain he was dead.

One stood above him with bloody knuckles. The one with clean hands unstrapped the prisoner, lifted his corpse from the chair and dragged it to the wall. He positioned its arms to the side so that the disfigured face was visible. He stepped back, but then approached to adjust limbs as if it were some form of macabre art. Which it was, probably, to the man standing above the dead insurgent. He smiled as blood continued to ooze from the terrorist's face. It made a nice pattern on the concrete floor and emphasized the suffering he experienced before he died.

"Next!" the one with bruised knuckles shouted.

Two guards dragged in a man in his underwear, threw him onto the chair recently vacated and secured his arms and legs with thick plastic ties, tightening them until they bit into his flesh. One of the interrogators moved the chair until it faced the battered man on the floor. The one with bloodied hands was mildly annoyed that he wore anything at all. It eased the process if the subject were as defenceless and vulnerable as possible. He hit the man in the chair with his right fist, and then with his left, and then again with his right. He let the man in the chair spit blood and teeth, catch his breath, and then hit him again. Right, left, right. The man spat more.

"Now that your mouth is clear, you can talk," the interrogator said. "Or maybe you need a wash?"

The guards that brought the prisoner in knew the cue for their next task. They entered the room with a rag and bucket of water. They set it next to the prisoner and left the room. The interrogator picked it up and dipped it into the bucket, rung out the excess fluid and wiped the prisoner's face with the rag. He tossed the cloth to the floor.

"I'm supposed to put this over your face and pour water until you think you're drowning, but that always struck me as stupid." He glared at the mirror lining one wall of the interrogation room with the two Defence Intelligence Agency agents watching on the other side of it.

"I say, if you want to make somebody think you are drowning them, you should just fucking drown them," he said. "Translate that, word for word. I will know if you don't because I speak your pig language."

A figure hidden in the corner of the room spoke. The man tied to the chair looked in the direction of the speaker, and then turned to face his interrogator. He spat, swearing in his own tongue.

"A bigger bucket!" the interrogator called. He stepped to the mirror. "Now. Full to the brim with icy cold water."

"Is he giving us an order?" a DIA agent asked.

"I think so," the other said.

"What should we do?"

"Get him his bucket of water," the first agent said.

A guard entered the room with a large pail of cold water and the interrogator walked behind his captive's chair and kicked it over. The man's knees slammed into the concrete floor, followed by his head. He blacked out for seconds but fought to maintain consciousness, gritting his teeth and focussing through the stars that filled his vision. The large bucket was placed beside his head. Water slopped onto his cheek. Then the two interrogators lifted the entire chair and submerged their prisoner's head in the bucket. The world grew dark as his struggles diminished. But before he was released from his imprisonment through death, they pulled him out of the water.

"It's just like the drone pilots," the DIA agent behind the glass said.

"What are you talking about?" the other asked.

"You know, they sit in some air-conditioned container in Las Vegas or somewhere and direct their deadly devices thousands of miles away from the actual death and destruction they inflict. They can blow up an Al Qaeda cell or a local market, write up a report, and go home to a dinner with the wife and kids in the suburbs."

"Your point?"

"Come on. The Airforce is experimenting with pilotless jet fighters. No pilots, if you can imagine. No human error, no black outs at high gravity turns or whatever. The jet can do what it was designed for and not be limited by a human body. Goes back to the same sick fucks controlling their drones in their cool containers. Automation. Wave of the future."

"That technology is way too complicated. That'd take decades. Pilotless jets." He shook his head as he laughed.

"That's exactly what I'm talking about."

"What the fuck are you talking about?"

"These guys," the first agent said, pointing through the glass. "These clones are automating our jobs. We should be in there extracting information. Instead, these things, with no moral compunction or restraint, are doing what we would never do. They've no doubt replaced every drone operator in the Nevada desert. No PTSD for these guys. Or leaks or documentaries. They don't whine about feeling guilty for killing women and children. And the Airforce doesn't need jet fighters on auto pilot anymore, because they got something cheaper. They don't have to risk real pilots when they have these guys. No mourning families, no body bags, but business as usual. Just keep producing ready grown human beings who will do whatever you train them for. And when you lose them, just make more."

"Maybe we're the drone operators here in your fucked up analogy. They get their hands dirty. We watch, collect the info and bring it to HQ."

"If only," the first agent said. "We're superfluous here. They're even giving us orders. Bring me water! Get me bucket! You realize that, don't you?"

"We process the data—"

"You don't think they can do that themselves? Train them right, they're smarter than us."

They stopped watching the interrogation in the adjoining room and stared at each other.

"Fuck that," the second agent said.

"Seriously," his colleague said. "You ever watch the movie, Apocalypse Now? It's a classic. You've seen this film. 'I love the smell of napalm in the morning' and all that shit. There's a scene where Colonel Kurtz is in awe of his enemy. This is Marlon Brando at the end of his career. A great bad guy, the renegade colonel who lives in the jungle with his own little army. But Kurtz tells Martin Sheen, who plays the guy sent to kill him, he tells him this story about he and his men passing through a village and inoculating all the children for something, small pox or measles, whatever. That little scar you have on your arm or leg? That was the one. But it's really just hearts and minds bullshit. Anyway, this VC patrol is following them, and when they get to the village, these VC gather all the children and hack off every limb that has a sign of inoculation. Kurtz and his men go back through the village later and find a pile of the small limbs. The VC had cut off every little arm with the mark and made a pile for the Americans to find."

"Why are you telling me this?" the first agent asked. "Those two in there could be the only ones they've made.'

"Are you that stupid? By the time they get around to sending two of these sadistic fucks to a hole like this—hell, I don't even know what country we're in—"

"Romania."

"—which you're not supposed to say out loud. If they're sending them here, you better believe they have a lot to spread around."

"So, what's the point of your story about the movie?"

"What Kurtz says," the agent replied. "What he says sums this up perfectly. Kurtz looks at the gruesome scene and this is what he takes away from it." He pointed to the glass window. "Kurtz isn't shocked by the pile of little arms. He isn't disgusted. He is impressed. Very goddamned impressed. He says that if he had a division of the men who had the will to do what he had just seen, to cut off the limbs of children, their own children ... He said with a division of those men, he would end the Vietnam War in a month." The agent stopped speaking and stared through the one-way glass.

"Those guys in there—" He tapped on the window separating them from the clones. "These all-American look a likes produced in some lab or factory stateside ... They're Kutz's division. Those guys are better than us. They make us look soft and retarded. They don't have some outdated morals nagging at the back of their brains, no memory of mother being disappointed, no judgemental all-seeing God to condemn them. They just do as they're trained."

The first agent shook his head, despite knowing his partner was right.

"Yeah, well, fuck that," he replied.

He unholstered his side arm and entered the interrogation room. The first shot killed the man who enjoyed ruining his hands against another man's skull. The second shot killed his twin. He motioned the interpreter close and together they lifted the chair upright. Then he stood above the man and recorded everything the terrified and confused prisoner had to say.

Gaia

B ut I don't get it. How can we be on a journey when we're just going in circles?

It's the time cycle you're hung up on. You have to slow down.

Slow down.

Yeah. Slow down to rock speed. Geologic time.

I still don't get it.

Yeah, you do. You just don't want to. We all fight it.

That we're going in circles?

But we're not, and you know it. We're travelling. It's just that its slow. Or not so slow. We've probably traveled over 100,000 light years since the last dinosaur died. Get over the need for instant gratification. All we're asked to do is our part.

I just ask for a purpose.

Of course you do. And you have it. Keep the ship sailing.

That sounds stupid.

No.

Yes. There is no ship.

We're on the ship.

We're on a planet. Orbiting a star. Round and round. Again and again. Year after year.

We're travelling through space. We're on the best designed generation ship that you could imagine. It has its own atmosphere, creates its own gravity, self-sustaining life support system... a home for every generation.

You're calling this a space ship?

That's what it is. It is traveling through space ...

Around and around a star for year after year after year ...

Which is itself travelling through space, as part of a galaxy that is travelling through space. In perfect symmetry, a marvel of frictionless technology. You just have to ...

Slow down?

You have no idea.

Enlighten me.

You'll never see the end of the voyage. I will never see the end of the voyage. Who knows what any of our ancestors might even look like when they reach the destination. Evolution keeps going just as we do, spiraling through the cosmos. But we'll make it. We'll get there.

Where?

I have no idea. But someday, we'll arrive. It's the whole point of why we're here.

Here?

Space ship Earth. Come on, you know this deep down somewhere. We all do. And we all know what we need to do. Just keep doing our part to keep the old gal flying. That, my friend, is the only thing you need to worry about.

Keep the planet going around the sun?

Yeah. Sounds simple, doesn't it?

Keep the planet going around the sun?

And make sure it remains habitable. Have something there when we arrive.

Arrive where?

I have no idea. And its irrelevant. It's not for us to know. It's not our fate. Our job, at this particular time, is just to keep her flying.

You're not making sense.

And now you're just being stupid. Or worse. Put your ego aside and do your job. Mother needs crew that understands their role. Ah, there you go. That little itch at the back of your head, that deep knowing. Take it in, there's no rush. But do, take it in. And double check the fuse on that C4. We want the whole oil rig to collapse.

Serving Time

I wait for the injection. Sentence had been rendered. I am to serve time. Seven consecutive life sentences. In legal verbiage life meant thirty years before parole. Short life, eh? Seven of those add up to a couple centuries. What was the point? Only I would be still be alive. Two hundred and some years in the future. Everything I knew, everybody I loved or hated or ... I don't know, wanted dead. Wanted to touch or love. Well, they would be long gone by then, wouldn't they? And I would be alone in a world I knew nothing about. A true stranger in a strange land. Punishment for ... something I did.

They wiped my memory. That was part of the sentence. Seven consecutive life sentences and a memory wipe. Part of the current thinking around rehabilitation, combined with advances in neurotechnology. It was possible, so they did it, cloaked in academic jargon. Once the sentence was served the felon could re-enter society with not only a clean record, but cleansed. Literally. A new person. I have no idea what they based their new philosophy on. Certainly not empirical data. I am, evidently, one of the first guinea pigs.

I rub my cheek and feel the smooth skin. They shaved me for some reason. I had a beard. I liked it. It made me feel … I can't remember what it made me feel. The shave happened after the wipe, so I know I had a beard. I also had long hair. Blond. Just stubble now. I don't know if that is part of the punishment. Cut off the lion's mane. Take away the power of mighty Samson by clipping his locks. I don't why I can remember that story if I can't even remember my name. Chained to columns, pulling down a building or something. I can't remember what made him do it. I must have really scared them. Not anymore.

I lay still as requested. I have no choice as I am strapped to a gurney. A nurse trying to look stern moves a tray close. She doesn't fool me. She is way out of her depth. And she is very pretty, she can't hide that behind a stern frown. I wink and she actually blushes. Maybe I'm handsome, I don't know. I feel a moment of pity for her, thrown into this situation. She should be wearing a summer dress, strolling through a field of fresh grass, flowers just peeking their shy blooms out of their buds, that time of spring that … Maybe they have already drugged me.

She avoids my eye as she takes the syringe and gently taps the barrel so any air bubbles float to the top. I want her to look at me, to see that it is okay, what she is doing. I deserve it, I guess. Not her. She should be among flowers. But she doesn't meet my gaze. Nobody does. So, I just lay back and wait as the needle pierces the skin and injects its solution. I won't be conscious for the next part, but they made sure I understood what would happen. It was important to them for some reason. Do I understand? Sign this form indicating that you understand. I feel a rage inside that I definitely do not understand. I feel an incredible urge to kill them all, to … images fade. They release an arm and put a pen in my hand. I sign the form with an 'x'.

I wasn't there, but I know what came next. Okay, so I was technically there, my body, at least. Once I was unconscious, I was moved to cryogenic chamber where my body was put in deep freeze. There I was to spend the next fifteen years. Half-life. I think that's a term used for radiation or chemistry or something. Half of a life sentence is what it means to them. At the end of fifteen years, I would be revived and spend one full day among the living. Well, not really. I would be able to see and breathe and think, alive, watched over by a solitary guard in the prison exercise grounds. Part of the rehabilitation, or the punishment. Sadistic sons of bitches.

The light hurts. I blink, then I stop and keep my eyes closed.

"Your eyes will adjust," I'm told, and feel glasses pushed onto my face.

I tentatively open my lids again and it is not as harsh. Sunglasses. What kindness. I look around and see concrete walls topped with barbed wire. The walls are easily twenty feet tall, so the barbed wire must be for Spiderman or some other freak. There are three guards at the top, each carrying a high-powered rifle. Not bolt action. Automatic. Their fingers are just outside the trigger guard and the safeties are not engaged. I am covered from three different angles. All of their eyes are on me. I do not know how I know this.

I can barely walk, and the guard helps me up, allowing me to lean against him as he leads me to a concrete bench. I sit and stare at my hands. I take a thumb and rub a palm. I stop and swap thumbs and palms before rubbing both hands together. I clap them, cherishing the sound. I look up. The guard is just a kid, probably fresh out of academy. But who knows, he might be my age. I don't even know who I am.

"You will feel disorientation at first," the kid says. "But that will pass. You will have eight hours in the exercise yard before being returned to stasis. During that time, you will be able to reflect on your punishment and future re-integration into society."

"Are you reading from a card?" I ask.

"They made me memorize it," he says. "They even made me practice. They pretended to wake up and made me ..."

He flinches when I laugh. The kid is scared shitless. I don't know why I want to comfort him. I shift a few inches away from him, place my hands beside me where he can see them, and just take in some air. It feels like sandpaper tearing away my insides, but I don't show it. I inhale with more care until it hurts less. After a few minutes of silence between us I ask if he has a name.

"I'm not supposed to ..." he stammers.

"It's okay, it's only us here," I say, ignoring the three guards with their guns above.

He looks up, and from where we came, and then finally at me.

"You got a name?" I ask again.

He is consulting regulations in his mind, but for some reason chooses to disregard them. "Abraham," he says. "Abe."

"Thanks, Abraham Abe," I answer. I offer my hand and he stares at it. No doubt another regulation, contact with prisoners and all that.

He surprises me by taking my hand. His grip is tentative but strong. I let my eyes leave his blue gaze and travel over his face. Brown hair, cut neat. Prison guard cut. His skin is smooth, yet untouched by disappointment or pain. No, that's not entirely fair. He has a strength in his jaw that's from experience and not chewing the shit. I wonder what he did before landing this particular job.

"What did you do before getting to work with me?" I ask, letting go of his hand. I can feel the guards above relax. And I am surprised when he answers truthfully.

"I worked the farm," Abe says. "Then the corporation swallowed it up, so I applied here."

"Congratulations," I answer. I didn't mean it sarcastically, but I think that's how he takes it. "I mean it," I say, "I don't know what it's like out there now, but having a steady job is a good thing still, isn't it?"

Abe kind of smiles. "It's a plus."

"You got a family?" I ask, and Abe starts to shut down.

"I'm really not supposed to be talking with you," he says. "Do you want to take exercise?" He points to the square of concrete and I can't help laughing.

"That's okay, Abe," I say. "As a matter of fact, I don't mind if we just talk a while and then you all can put me back on ice."

He sat and stared at his own hands for a good five minutes and I sat beside him in silence until he finished.

"I'm not allowed to talk about the outside," he finally says.

"I don't even know who I am," I say. "I have no interest in what's out there, so you're safe."

We sat in another silence that seemed to sort more than any words could. Then I broke it.

"You got a woman? Someone special?" I ask.

And he smiled, showing deep dimples. "Yeah," he says.

"She good to you?" I ask. For some reason that seemed important to me.

"She is," he says, and a glint in his eye made me pry more.

"And?"

"We got a kid on the way," he says, grinning.

"That's fantastic, Abe. I'm sure you'll make a great dad."

I had nothing to base that on, just a vibe. But he stiffened as I say it, remembering where he was or maybe who I was, whoever that may have been. He stood and took a step back from the bench. He placed his hands behind his back.

"Your time is running short," he tells me. "You may want to take advantage of the yard."

I nod. "Thanks, Abe," I say. "I think I might do that." And I stood and walked the small circuit while the guards above followed my every step and Abe waited by the door. Finally, the time came to an end.

The light hurts. I keep my eyes closed remembering what is happening. I am being awoken. Defrosted. Revived. Or whatever it's called.

"Your eyes will adjust," I am told. I recognize the voice.

"Abe," I say, eyes still closed. "Nice to see you again."

He doesn't answer, but I feel his hand on my arm. I blink as I sit up. The light burns, but blinking helps. My eyelids seem to work when I want them and stay open instead of involuntarily flutter. I stand. My legs don't want to respond as quickly as I want and I lurch forward like Frankenstein's monster. I don't know who that is. But I must, somehow. The dead re-animated. Am I dead? No, remember. I am a prisoner revived for a short time as some sort of torture/punishment/rehabilitation experiment. Abe leads me to a concrete bench in front of a small exercise yard. Four walls of concrete, topped with barbed wire and patrolled by three guards. The guards are different, as are their weapons. I am not familiar with their weapons. But I am sure they are lethal.

I inhale carefully. "Thank you," I say to Abe, not knowing why.

"You will feel disorientated at first, but that will pass," he says.

I laugh and put a hand on his thigh as I do. "We've done this before," I say. I remove my hand before he does. My vision returns. He's not a kid anymore but a man. He's got a cop moustache, though I don't know what that means. He's a man, straight down to the worry lines radiating from the corners of his eyes.

"How's the kid?" I ask after a silence.

He seems surprised at my question, that I would know anything about him, but I don't have much to remember, and our last conversation happens to be a very large part of that. For me, it was only yesterday. Then it dawns that for Abe fifteen years has passed.

"Kid?" he asks. "Oh. She's great."

"That sounds like you have more than one," I say.

He glances up at the guards on the walls, shakes his head, and meets my gaze. He smiles. "Yeah," he says. "More than one."

"Go on," I say, "Give it to me."

He's grinning and shaking his head. "Do you want to take advantage of the yard? Stretch your legs?"

"Fuck that," I answer. 'What's the point? Kids, huh? How many?"

He relaxed his posture, even smiled. "Three," he says. "Cassie is a sophomore now. Real smart girl."

"Cassie," I repeat. He doesn't seem to mind me saying her name and I'm not sure why he should.

"Josh is thirteen. That's a tough age," he offers. "And Toby will be ten next month."

"Wow," I say. "You got a houseful."

"That's an understatement," Abe answers. He is no longer the timid young recruit but an experienced corrections officer.

"How's the missus?" I ask.

"She's good." He smiles. "She holds us all together."

"I'm glad to hear that," I answer. And I am. People got to stick together when there's kids involved. I feel it more than remember it.

"Say," I suggest, "Why don't you walk with me along these four walls and tell me what family life is like?"

I am surprised when he agrees with a nod. We rise and start to the first small circuit and talks about Cassie and her high school soft-ball team crashing out at regionals, Josh wanting a new hover-bike, whatever that is, and Toby having trouble with his temper at school. Jil—that's his wife's name—says she wants to homeschool him, but neither of them has the education or the time that'd take. They hardly get by on both their salaries and one of them staying at home all day with a ten-year-old is just out of the question.

I eat up his words like sponge cake. They satisfy a deep need, but leave me wanting more. I remember I am being punished. Maybe this is it. We finish a circuit and Abe almost apologizes when he tells me my time is up. He doesn't flinch when I pat his back and thank him. I appreciate that he doesn't ask what for. I want to tell him to give my regards to the family but still know what is and isn't appropriate. We shake hands before I lie on the gurney.

My eyes adjust to the bright light and I see Abe. His moustache is gone, replaced by grey stubble. His hair is thinner, streaked with grey. Well, grey streaked with what colour his hair used to be. He lends a hand and I stand.

"You will feel disorientation at first," he says. "But that will pass." And he laughs. We walk to the bench in the exercise yard without speaking.

"You're looking older, Abe," I say after we have stared at the sky for several minutes. We both ignore the guards above. The barbed wire has been replaced with something that glows and what they hold in their hands does not resemble anything I would recognize as a weapon. But I know it is deadly.

"I am older," he answers. I realize for the first time that he has never said my name, not even a number.

I don't really care what my name it is. "How's Jil?" I ask. It was only yesterday we were talking about his homelife.

"She is good," Abe answers. "Had a bit of scare with the big C, but medicine nowadays can take care of anything that can throw at us."

"Glad to hear it," I say.

"She's looking forward to my retirement," Abe adds.

"Wow. Congratulations. When is that going to happen?"

"I actually put it off a few months so I can be here," he says. "See you one more time. Round off my career. Complete a circle, so to speak."

I am touched. I really am. "Well, thanks," I tell him. I don't know what else to say. He wears a soft smile and nods his understanding. We begin to walk along the walls, completing a circuit before realizing we had started. He's a grandfather, Cassie no longer concerned with softball losses. He's looking forward to being around to be more a part of their lives. They moved to the coast and Jil and he have already put the house on the market. He laughed when I mentioned Toby and school troubles, saying the boy was teaching math at a local community college. I remember the middle boy's name. Josh works at Luna City and they only see him on the screen. Abe clams up as if he's told me too much, but then scans the sky and points at the moon.

"If you look real close, you might see a light," he tells me. "It'll no doubt be bigger the next time you wake."

He leads me out of the small yard and to a waiting gurney. He offers his hand and I hold it. "It's been a pleasure," I tell him, and he simply nods.

"You will feel disorientation at first," a voice I don't recognize says. "But that will pass. You will have eight hours in the exercise yard before being returned to stasis. During that time—"

"Yeah," I say. "This isn't my first rodeo."

"During that time," the voice continues, "You will be able to reflect on your punishment and future re-integration into society."

"By the book," I mutter.

I slowly open my eyes to see a face that isn't Abe's. He isn't smiling. He doesn't look like he can. My gaze moves from him to the room and the weak pink light outside of it. It's all different. I move my legs from the gurney and almost fall, push myself away from the floor and feel the gurney bite into my back. The guard stands, not smiling but seemingly amused. Something is definitely off.

"Why do I feel funny?" I ask.

"Probably the weaker gravity," the guard says. "You won't have time to get used to it."

"Where am I?"

"You have been re-located to the Secure Holding Facility at Hellas Planitia." He doesn't say any more about the move or the place, but adds: "You have eight hours in the exercise yard before being returned to stasis."

He places his hands behind his back and stands beside a wall. I move towards the exercise 'yard' filled with pink light. There is a bench for sitting, four walls to walk around. But there are no guards atop the wall, no barbed wire or weapons. There is just a glass dome. Outside the dome the sky is pink. I stand staring at it, mouth open. A small shape passes quickly from west to east. I know how Dorothy felt. I am not in Kansas anymore. I turn to the guard but he is only paying attention to me peripherally. Questions would be wasted on him.

Answers would be wasted on me. I sit and stare at the strange sky for hours.

"You will feel disorientation at first." This voice is different. I let it intone the rest of the script. I get up carefully.

"Thank you," I say the guard, already assuming a stance against a wall. "I'll just be out here," I add as I move to small yard.

The bench is waiting for me. I sit and watch the sky through the dome. A light in the east moves slowly. It isn't a star. A moon? I try to remember how many moons Mars had, if that is where I am. I can't.

The guard drones through the notice that I am quite familiar with. Eight hours. Reflect. He sounds as if he's saying it for the thirtieth time this month. Maybe he is. Now that's a thought. He is little more talkative than the others. He tells me about his tour, grindingly long and uneventful, sold on the pitch and signing up. See new worlds! He even laughs and gestures at the yard and the glass dome. Exciting, huh? But he'll go back home a lot richer than he left. Or he'll stay and take a better job and live in an apartment much bigger than anything he would get on Earth. Yeah, they shipped you off as soon as they could, he says before I can ask. He declines joining me at the bench, where I watch a sky swirling with clouds of dust.

I lose count of my 'periods of reflection'. I forget when human guards are replaced with machines. They look a little more humanoid each time. They don't talk much, just answer questions very factually. The shape above this exercise yard is unmistakable. It is massive, taking up half the dome, bands of browns and tans and dirty white swirling around it. I turn to the machine. I seem to have outlived any human willing to keep track of me. I guess I'm immortal. Or worse. I think about that young kid, Abe, long dead. His kids are dead. Their kids dead. Anybody that ever remembered him are dead. Except me.

I ask questions and the machine answers. Galileo Penal Colony. Ganymede. No. No, it answers again, there is no return. Yes, there are humans on Ganymede. I will join them at the resettlement community upon my release. One half life before release to general population at Heliopolis. That is the name of the human resettlement community. As part of an astronomical tradition, all names on the moon have origins in ancient Greek mythology. After a few more answers that only make me feel utterly depressed, I don't know what to say or ask and stare at the machine in silence.

"Do you have any further queries?" it asks.

"Um, no, I guess not," I answer.

"You have eight hours to reflect on your punishment and future re-integration into society," it reminds me. I sit on the lone bench in the yard and gaze at the massive planet above me.

THE SHACKLETON MOMENT

Jens and Lassen gazed at the planet below. *Shackleton*. Deep greens and blacks patterned the surface. Bands of white cloud circled the hemispheres. Ice caps covered the poles. As the ship fell into orbit, the two men spent most of the watch simply gazing at the screen, watching the world beneath them slowly turn.

Jens was first to fill the silence on the bridge. "I haven't seen green for so long."

"That's what broke their hearts, man," Lassen said.

"What do you mean?"

"You know the story. There are other rocks that claim *Shack* status, but it was really this one. This is where humanity gave up."

"It's beautiful," Jens said.

"Which is why it hurt so much," Lassen said. "Imagine—almost a century searching for a ... who knows what they were looking for. Another Earth? Someplace to replace the one they trashed? And all they find is lifeless rock after lifeless rock. Air too thin or poisonous to breathe. Soil too poor. Nothing alive, not even a nanobe. Desperate suckers like those below would still take the chance, living under domes or deep in caves, but it was here that ended all that for most. Where a planet of billions gave up hope and stopped looking. Come on," Lassen said. "You know the story."

"Yeah, who doesn't?" Jens said. "We finally admit that there is no Planet B and we cleaned up what we had."

"That's funny, coming from you, Mr. Garbage Man," Lassen said. "You used to work in collections on Earth, didn't you? Scouring the seas for plastics? Take a look. This rock is why you lost your job. Or why you had one in the first place." He laughed. "Collecting garbage on a planet newly committed to no waste. Your days were numbered from the beginning."

"The pickings were getting slim out there," Jens admitted.

"It's because of this planet," Lassen said.

They both lapsed into silence, watching the clouds shift in the currents of the upper atmosphere.

"Clouds, rain, an atmosphere that's almost breathable," Lassen said. "Put yourself in those guy's suits. They've probably been Stepping for over a decade, folding space and travelling across the galaxy. Dead planet after dead planet. Rock after rock. Then they see green. They get into their flier and descend. The green gets closer. Closer. And it turns out to be rock. Green rock. What kind of cosmic joke is that? There was a very high suicide rate on the Steps back to Earth. Those folks literally gave up. Read *Stepping Out*, by the captain of one of the early exploratory ships. Teal has a copy. The captain of the exploratory vessel kept a journal. Reads like an extended suicide note, which I guess it was. But worth the read if you're going to stay out here."

"Thanks, I will," Jens said.

"You know the real Shackleton story?" Lassen asked. Sharing long watches with the first mate had led to a grudging yet mutual respect, but Jens had not heard his superior as talkative as this.

"Antarctic explorer. Ship stranded. Rescues his men," Jens offered.

"That's a hell of a story," Lassen said. "But not that one. You really need to read more."

"Go on, tell me." Jens settled back into his chair.

"Get me a coffee first."

"Aye, aye sir!" Jens returned in a few minutes with two mugs.

"Back in the day—"

"That's a great start," Jens interrupted.

"Quiet in the front," Lassen said. "Back in the day, nobody had reached the south pole. It's hard to imagine now—no airlift, they walked! Across the ice for weeks, wearing waxed canvas, carrying everything, trudging across a frozen wasteland for weeks. Shackleton was an incredible leader. You need to read about Shackleton if you want to really understand about leading. He was well on his way to reaching the pole, claiming the prize, being a national hero. Fame and glory. But somewhere along the way he listened to that small, quiet voice in the back of his head, and he did the math. He knew he could reach the pole, be the first to reach it, knew the prize was his for the taking. He would be remembered forever, immortalized in history. But do you know what else he knew?"

Jens opened his hands and shrugged.

"He saw that, while he could reach the pole, he wouldn't make it back. Not just him, but the men under his command," Lassen continued. "Think about the story you're familiar with. Ice crushes his ship, and his crew is stranded, so he takes five handpicked men and sails a dinghy hundreds of miles across treacherous seas, climbs mountains, finds another ship, and months later rescues the crew he left back on the ice. Every single one of them.

"On that earlier expedition, the one aiming for the pole, Shackleton had the prize in his grasp. He would have been known forever as the man who conquered the pole. Know what he did? He turned around. His men tried to argue with him, but he would have none of it. So back they trudged across the ice, failures, but alive. Now, Amundsen was the first to reach the pole, a few years later. Who was the second?" Lassen asked.

"Scott," Jens answered. "I grew up outside of Christchurch in New Zealand. Last stop to Antarctica."

"Good for you," Lassen said. "And correct. Scott was considered a hero. He reached the pole. What else did Scott do, Jens?"

"He died."

"Exactly. When Scott reached the same point as Shackleton, where Sir Ernest turned around, he felt proud when he passed it, like it was some kind of achievement. He beat Shackleton! Scott had a goal, and he was single-minded in wanting to reach it. So, he carried on. He reached the pole only to find that Amundsen had beaten him by a month. The Norwegian left him a nice note, too. Then, Scott turned around and walked he and his men to death on the way back.

"This is it," Lassen said, gesturing to the view screen. "This is the moment when we listened to the voice in our heads, the voice Scott ignored. The voice Shackleton listened to. People have come up with lots of reasons why Scott didn't make it back. Not enough protein for the walk, or not the right type of nourishment to pull their sleds day after day after day, the whole party getting weaker and weaker. Through it all, they continued to drag sleds full of rock samples, too. Lots of analogies to draw from there, don't you think? And as a result, he lost his men and he lost his life. Scott was heralded as a hero at the time. But we know better now.

"And here we are," Lassen said. "The Shackleton Moment. When humanity chose to return while they still could, when they still had the chance, when they could salvage and clean up where they lived."

"The *Shack*," Jens said.

"That's right," Lassen agreed. "You ever see your grandparents again, you can tell them about what you saw and say another thank you. That was a gutsy generation."

"As they like to tell us," Jens said.

"Believe them. They could have kept trashing and grasping, but instead, they became the generation that finally, *finally*, took responsibility. My oma was on the streets, stopping the tanks with her bare tits. I didn't believe her when I was a kid, and then she showed me the pictures. Standing in the street with her shirt pulled up. She was a very pretty young woman. And very brave. But that was happening all over Europe and North America. Even in China."

Lassen leaned forward and peered into the view screen. "See that light down there?"

Jens searched the surface and saw a pinprick of light in a sea of green.

"Computer, magnify," Lassen said.

The image on the screen increased in size. The light became a clear star on the green surface.

"Magnify and continue until command to stop," Lassen told the computer. The light grew until what was a habitation dome became blurrily apparent.

"Stop magnification," Lassen said. "Living under a dome. Their entire world, just a few miles in diameter—unless they suit up with an aspirator. And the settlers keep coming. Who would choose that kind of life?"

"You live in a lead lined ship surrounded by the cold vacuum of space," Jens said. "I don't think you're one to criticize."

"True, true," Lassen said. "I'm not criticizing, just amazed. There are two more domes on the other side of the planet. McMurdo, mostly American, keeping with the theme of Antarctic bases. And Vostok. This is probably like Siberia in winter to the Russians, only much farther away from their worthless rulers. There are truckloads of Russians out here.

"But there's not a lot of Russians at Scott," Lassen added. "They tend to stick to their part of the planet. You'll see all that tomorrow when you go down."

"You're not going?" Jens asked. "Bit of R and R, a bit of drinking yourself blind?"

"I'll just watch from here, thank you very much," Lassen answered. "I've seen too many mining colonies. Depressing affairs." He lifted his empty coffee mug and inspected the inside before handing it over to Jens.

"How about a little milk in it this time?" he asked.

Jens took the mug and rose.

"A little milk it is," he said before he left the bridge.

THE SHIP OF ALL WORLDS

Female Number Two felt a strain in her left calf but continued to run. It would pass. Pain was temporary. She had ten minutes remaining at her current pace before cool down mode started. Grabbing the small towel hanging from the controls she wiped her brow and increased the incline of the machine. She clenched the towel in her fist as her thigh muscles burned and her lungs screamed. This wasn't part of her fitness program. She was improvising, responding to an inner urge that frightened her. Frightened, but also excited.

She breathed hard as cool down mode initiated and the treadmill decreased speed. Walking at a brisk pace, she wiped sweat from her face and tossed the damp towel in the direction of the cleaning receptacle. When she could, Female Number Two breathed through her nose, long deep inhales and quick exhales. As she began to feel dizzy and the world grew dark, she grasped the handrails and sucked in air. It was a little game she recently started playing at the end of workouts. Were it not for the possibility of physical injury if she completely passed out, she would keenly sink into the black nothingness of unconsciousness, just for the experience. Or so she thought. She never tried it, but the idea was intriguing.

Despite the small changes to her physical fitness routine and brief experiments with asphyxia, Female Number Two was a creature of routine. It was all she knew. Bred and trained for one purpose, she was, until recently, completely intent on its fulfilment. As the treadmill slowed to a complete stop, she stepped off, picked up the sweat-soaked towel from the deck and placed it in the receptacle. There it joined other soiled garments to be washed and dried for reuse. Another closed system in their closed world. Everything recycled and reused, as there was no replacement. That small world sped through space, farther and farther from Earth. There was no possibility for replacing anything.

Female Number Two opened the door of the gym the same time Female Number One arrived for her training session. Female Number Two stood in front of the other woman, whom she had known since gestation. The smell of her own sweat filled her nostrils but she tilted her nose to catch the scent of the other woman. She felt an urge to touch her arm. To press her open mouth against the soft neck of the other, touch her sweet flesh with tongue and taste her goodness. These thoughts were new and strange, and Female Number Two liked them. She longed to grow closer with her crewmate but knew waiting would bring fullness.

It was in the book. She read and believed it. The book was strange and found buried at the bottom of her gear locker. It was not an accident that it was there. Female Number Two was trained to be meticulous about supplies. All stores on the ship were stowed by technicians, who knew that the crew would double-check every item they placed on board. On an eight-year voyage, nothing was left to chance, even if that was only a half-filled container of drink solution that was listed as full. The first safety redundancy was not trusting anything to ground crew. The second was knowing everything about equipment and supplies. There was no room for error, nor extra space for non-essentials. Which is why Female Number Two was perplexed when she lifted the paperback book from her own stores.

The book was full of mystery and confusion. It was like nothing she had ever read. Books and information programs contained essential knowledge. That was their purpose. Everything studied was directed at the successful completion of the mission. Engineering. Biology. Particle physics. Nuclear science. Mathematics. Astrophysics. She and her five crewmates trained for three years together, every waking hour of every day, with a single focus: Crew the *Cronus* to Titan, Saturn's largest moon. Three females and three males, produced for one purpose. To go further than any human had ever gone before.

Female Number Two never knew distraction. Her thoughts never strayed from the goal. All of the time spent after her gestation was spent developing her mind and body. There were no minutes spare to question, or wonder, or even think beyond the parameters of the mission. She had neither capacity nor inclination to lose focus. But the book caused her to ... she wasn't sure she knew the word to describe what she felt, but when not on duty, she turned her full and well-developed attention to the text. While life on the ship maintained a rigor and routine, now there were no watchers from mission control, and the pressure to preform was removed. Only once the six were aboard the *Cronus*, every day that took them farther from Earth also permitted a repose none of them were previously allowed to experience.

After her workout, Female Number Two made her way to the ablutions unit. She breathed rapidly as she walked along the corridor of the great ring that continually rotated around the *Cronus'* cylindrical body. Her breathing wasn't caused by exertion in the third of a gravity created through the movement of the ring. It was through excitement. She passed the living quarters, the mess and galley, the science lab, the communications room, deliberately taking the long way to prolong her anticipation.

Female Number Two reached the showers and stood naked under the warm water. She closed her eyes and thought of Female Number One, letting her hand touch her own breasts, to travel slowly down her flat stomach until reaching her moist crotch. The touch was a new sensation, one she never knew was possible until reading The Book. There was so much of that in The Book. It was shocking to read at first, but then Female Number Two found pleasure in the words. And she experimented on herself, growing closer with herself. She decided it was nice. More than nice, it was a goodness. Female Number Two gasped as she finished, the warm water of the shower continuing to pour over her satiated body. She wanted to share with her crew mates, but grokked that waiting was required.

The book Female Number Two held in her hands was a text very unlike any she had studied before. Written by the historian, Robert A Heinlein, it covered a period of Earth history involving the return of a human child raised on Mars, named Michael Valentine Smith, sometimes called 'The Man from Mars.' He was a Stranger in a Strange Land. The history was very well named. The more Female Number Two read, she felt like a stranger in a land she only thought she understood. But now she realized she knew nothing of the planet they left behind. She already read the text twice, and her highly developed skills of recall meant that she could recite the text verbatim. She flicked through pages at random, glimpses of Michael's life after his return to Earth, his growing understanding of humanity, and his great teachings to those willing to listen.

In preparing for their mission, Female Number Two and her crewmates never ventured beyond the training facility. They never watched stereovision of the outside world, they never associated with any person not essential to the success of the *Cronus* and their voyage to Titan. So Female Number Two savored the window smuggled onboard and the view of the world they had left behind. She joined Gillian Boardman as she and Michael sneaked out of his hospital confinement, swam in the water of life in Jubal Harshaw's pool, and struggled with Michael to grok the confusing species he was a part of. What was grokking? Female Number Two had been using the word more freely, at least to herself, and although understanding of the term increased, she still didn't feel like she fully 'grokked' it. Knowing a thing intimately. Intuitively. Empathetically. Sympathetically. A merging and blending of observer and observed.

"What was grokking?" Jubal Harshaw mused in the pages of Heinlein's history. *He had been using the word for a week*, Heinlein recounted, *and he didn't grok it.*

Female Number Two continued to study, knowing, as Michael taught, that waiting would bring fullness. Understanding would come. Through the pages of the text, Female Number Two moved out of Jubal's nest with Michael and Gillian, learning with them as they worked various jobs that Female Number Two could barely understand. She joined the two, and Dorcas and Anne and Myriam and Duke and Larry and others as Michael began his mission of helping humanity realize its potential, founding the Church of All Worlds, teaching the Martian language so all could grok and understand their true nature. Like all of his Inner Circle, Female Number Two did not cry when Michael was killed by the Fosterite mob. Like the others in his nest, she grokked that fullness was achieved. It was time for his nest to create their own churches, to spread the Martian wisdom among humanity.

Female Number Two recognized the book was more than mere history. It was a blueprint. A primer. A holy text. During her first reading she felt anger—a new emotion, but as she began to grok, she accepted and cherished the feeling before letting it go. She, and her nestlings on the *Cronus*, were kept ignorant, deprived worse than a prisoner in a maximum-security jail, never allowed to gaze out of any window, real or metaphorical. And yet here they were now, given an opportunity to become fully human. To become a new species, as Michael encouraged. *Homo Superior*. She offered gratitude to the laboratory that grew them, the attendants who trained them, and the technicians that sent them on their way. She placed a hand reverently on the text by Heinlein and inhaled slowly, clearing her mind and beginning to practice as Michael taught his water brothers to practice. She knew no Martian, the book itself contained none of the mother tongue, but she increasingly grokked like a Martian.

Many of Michael's water brothers first had to overcome the limitations imposed upon them by the cultures in which they were raised and brainwashed. Religious cosmology shaped their understanding of the universe. Heavens, hells, gods, devils. Morals defined not only what one could do, but even what they could think. Female Number Two had no such indoctrination. She began each session by focusing on the book beside her. As Michael taught, "First you grok a thing, then you grok it to—" Michael was explaining to Jubal how he could make a large box levitate. Female Number Two decided to make The Book raise in front of her and open to one of her favorite passages, where Michael is in Ben's apartment shortly after his escape with Gillain Boardman from Bethesda Hospital. Michael steps onto Ben's living floor, a carpet of soft grass, and is delighted at the invitation he receives from each blade ...

Female Number Two read the words as they floated in front of her and smiled. She then had the book close itself and settle back to the deck. She closed her eyes and turned inward as Michael taught, examining her body, taking her awareness deep inside, offering nourishment to each cell. She analyzed the chemicals released by the contraceptive implant injected into her arm and she neutralized them. With increasing control of her own body, she knew that conception of new life would occur only when she decided it was appropriate. No invasive device would impede or interfere with that. Focusing on another implant, she grokked wrongness. Its chemicals encouraged docility and compliance. She viewed the small device from every angle until she cherished all aspects of its clever technology, even loving its compactness and power. And then she made it go away.

Michael did that to things grokked as wrong. Like weapons. And people. Michael first demonstrated this ability in Ben's apartment, when men showed up to kill Gillian and bring Michael back to the hospital. One of the men struck Gillian. Michael reached in an odd fashion towards the man, and then the man was not there any longer. When the other man threatened them with a gun, Michael reached out and that man was gone. At Father Jubal's nest, Michael demonstrated and tried to explain. Jubal needed to watch the tape of the event in slow motion, but still could not grasp what was happening. He watched the item grow smaller and smaller until it disappeared. Female Number Two was getting better at doing this.

Michael also taught that it was possible to craft one's body. He did it himself, building muscle rapidly at Father Jubal Harshaw's house. Female Number Two wanted to increase the mass of her body, to be more like Anne, whom the historian described as 'pleasantly plump'. She knew she could do it, but waiting was required. Her nestlings needed to grok before any outward change was made. However, at that moment, Female Number Two decided that she no longer liked what she was named. Indeed, she realized that what she was called was not a name at all. Nobody in the history recounted by Robert A Heinlein was known by a gender or a number.

"From now on, I will be known as Anne," she pronounced to the empty room.

So determined, she let her awareness leave her body as taught by the Man from Mars and let her disembodied mind enter the corridor. She did this before within her own quarters, gaining confidence and skill with practice, watching her body from above, or explore the small cabin without hinderance of body. This time she wanted to try something more. Flowing through the accommodation ring she entered the quarters of Male Number One. For what seemed a long time, because she had slowed her sense of time, Anne cherished the form of the sleeping man. Then she entered his mind and spoke.

Thou art God, She said. *May you never thirst.*

Thou art God. Anne liked the concept. She grokked it with more fullness, recounting a passage:

"Jubal, my brother, you were ask me," Michael explained, "'Who made the world?' and I did not have words why I did not grok it rightly to be a question. I have been thinking words."

"So?"

"You told me, 'God made the world.'"

"No, no!" Harshaw said. "I told you that, while religions said many things, most of them said, 'God made the world.' I told you that I did not grok the fullness, but that 'God' was the word that was used."

"Yes, Jubal," Mike agreed. "Word is 'God'," he added, "You grok."

"I must admit I don't grok."

"You grok," Smith repeated firmly. "I am explain. I did not have the word. You grok. Anne groks. I grok. The grasses under my feet grok in happy beauty. But I needed the word. The word is God."

"Go ahead."

Mike pointed triumphantly at Jubal. "Thou art God!"

Thou art God, Anne whispered in the sleeping man's mind. Male Number One continued to dream. A woman offered him a glass of water, holding in the gesture a promise of eternal devotion. She also had something beside the water to share, something physical and yet also of emotion. He grew erect as he dreamed and smiled as he slept.

Anne left his room and went to that of Female Number Two, gazing for several moments at her sleeping form. Then she drifted through the bulkhead and found Male Number Three on the bridge with Female Number Three. Male Number Two was in the galley eating. Female Number One was drying herself after her shower. Into each mind she said the same: *Thou art God. May you never thirst*, and she left an anticipation of more to come—knowledge, growth, fullness. If they remembered anything from her subconscious visit, it would be anticipation. And that their crewmate was no longer called by a gender or number, but a name. Anne.

Anne gave the contraband book to Male Number One, who read and memorized it before passing it to Female Number One, who sent it on its way throughout the crew after cherishing and memorizing every word. As each read the history, Anne was with them, helping them use the wisdom within. Anne encouraged her crew mates to grok an item and lift or move it. When the men came to re-capture Michael and he sent them 'away', Anne shared what she understood about wrongness and how to make nothingness of it. To know that something is not right and to take right action. The females sent their contraceptive implants away, and all rid themselves of the mood-altering chemical devices.

When Anne intuited it was time, she called her brothers and sisters to the messroom. They sat around the oval dining table that held a pitcher of clear water and one glass. Anne stood and poured water into the glass and held it aloft, just as Michael celebrated the water ceremony with those he loved.

"With this water we grow ever closer," she said. "By sharing it, we become one. We become whole." Anne took a sip from the glass. "By sharing water we become brothers. We become one. May you never thirst."

She handed the glass to Male Number One, who took the name Jubal. He drank, and as he passed the water to Female Number One, who claimed the name Myriam, he said, "Thou art God."

Myriam took the glass and held it reverently. The red tint of her hair reflected off the clear liquid. Like Anne, she was adept at controlling her body and shaping it to fit her desires. She sipped the water, savoring every molecule as it became a part of that body.

"Share water," she said to Duke, formerly labeled Male Number Two.

Duke closed his eyes and took a sip before passing the glass to Female Number Three, now called Dorcas, her darkened skin and deep brown hair setting her apart from her clone sisters and demonstrating mastery over her body.

"Never thirst," she said before handing the glass to Male Number Three, now known as Larry.

After the last of the nest shared water, Anne stood again and spread her arms wide. Once water was shared, they were bound to one another. There was no mine, his, or hers. All was shared, including their bodies. One moment her body was covered by the mission flight suit.

The next moment her full beauty was on display and all of her water brothers admired the ample sculpting.

"Michael told us that the actual joining and blending of two physical bodies with simultaneous merging of souls in shared ecstasy of love, giving and receiving and delighting in each other, made the planet Earth rich and wonderful. It does not exist on Mars, where there is no division such as man and woman. This division is a gift. As Michael explained to Jubal on page six hundred of the sacred history, 'until a person, man or woman, has enjoyed this treasure bathed in the mutual bliss of having minds linked as closely as bodies, that person is still as virginal and alone as if he had never copulated.'"

Anne smiled warmly at the faces gazing up at her. Her only experience at lovemaking was with herself, but she felt a deep confidence to press on. "I invite you now, my water brothers, to dispense with your virginity and join me in experiencing a true goodness, in becoming whole."

Jubal stood, and in the same way as Anne, shed his flight suit, sending it to wherever such things went. Myriam and Dorcas and Duke and Larry stood, their clothing similarly disappearing. Anne left her place at the table and took Jubal's hand. He took Duke's, who took Myriam's, until all made a chain that followed their priestess into the viewing room. The floor was covered with their bedding, moved there by thought while she shared water with her brothers. Once all were inside, she took Jubal's face in her hands and kissed him as taught by Michael, with all of her attention. Then she pulled Myriam towards her and offered her lips. The others, rather than spectate, reached for the water brother nearest and gave them their fullest consideration.

Anne returned to Jubal and pulled him down and on top of her. She opened her legs and her mind and they grew close. The others took their lead, paired off and shared, and when finished rolled or stepped over and continued the growing closer with a new partner.

"Thou art God!" Anne shouted in ecstasy, and heard herself answered by each of her water brothers, a mental echo that filled her with power.

Thou art God!

We must refrain from making clothing go away. It is a finite resource.

You don't seem to bother with them much, Anne said. Thought. Conveyed.

Jubal smiled. One hand rested on a hip, the other hung loosely beside a thigh. Were he made of marble, he would have been at home beside Michelangelo's David. Although cutting the physical fitness routine out of his time table, his body was toned and muscles sculpted. It was how he wanted to look, so he thought that body into being. And it gave him extra time for grokking. There was much to grok.

That is not the point. We must manage our resources wisely.

True, Anne agreed.

Practice the removal of things only on what is a wrongness. Like the hormone implants in our bodies, or the contraceptive devices imposed upon the females.

And the remote control of our vessel? Anne asked.

I grok it is a wrongness, Jubal said. *As do you.*

It is now disabled, she replied. *We control our destiny.*

Mission control has tried to make contact again, Dorcas interrupted.

Did you respond?

No. I made them go away.

You what? Anne and Jubal exclaimed. They heard laughter in their minds.

I turned off the communication console, Dorcas replied. *The humans at mission control are still corporate, but now they will not pester us with questions or orders.*

You have acted wisely, Jubal told her. He closed his eyes and tilted his head to the left. *What is it, Larry?* He asked.

I sense a wrongness, Larry said.

Continue.

According to the historian Robert A Heinlein, when the Envoy *left Earth for that dangerous first mission to Mars, it was followed by all of humanity. And when the* Champion *was sent years later to discover the fate of the* Envoy, *there was even greater global interest. All knew about Michael, how he was born on Mars and raised by the Martians after the death of his parents. His return to Earth was the greatest story of the era. He was a celebrity.*

And the wrongness you grok? Jubal asked.

We were created for a mission to take us even farther than Mars, and yet ...

Larry's thoughts hung within all the crew as he paused, and in the space between words each grokked the depth of his reasoning. There was no fanfare at their departure. There were no new faces, no media, no stereovision. The world outside of the training facility was denied those within, at least the six created for the mission. Each felt an emotion fused with resentment and anger and loss. Each examined the feelings within themselves as if it were a physical object, a tumor or cyst. And when each became one with every aspect of it, when each knew the emotion thoroughly, they let it go.

None know of our mission, or of us, Myriam said.

None will know when we return, Duke said. *If we are meant to return.*

The water brothers felt Jubal stretching the sense of time and they joined with him. By the ship's chronometer mere seconds passed, but to the crew one hour stretched into another and another.

We are only eggs, Anne said, and each reflected on her words. Michael called himself an egg when he realized how much he did not grok. A Martian youngling, lacking in experience and wisdom. But the teachings of the Man from Mars came naturally to them. Unencumbered by culture and its preconceptions or imposed ideas of morality, they were trained from gestation to focus the mind. They turned their open and concentrated consciousness to absorbing Michael's wisdom. They were already unrecognizable from the crew that left Earth. They were so much more. And yet they all knew they were merely scratching at their true potential.

We are only eggs, they agreed.

After a long period of silence, Jubal spoke. *We must learn from the Old Ones.*

I have reached out, but they remain silent, Duke said.

The Old Ones are wise. We must assume their reticence is purposeful, Anne said.

Waiting is, each agreed.

Michael was the fountain and source of all knowledge of the water of life, Myriam said. *He left the language with the Inner Circle of the church. They can teach us and help us grow as Michael desired.*

There was a pause that lasted mere minutes on the ship, yet allowed the nest to grok for days upon the implications of Myriam's words. When Jubal spoke, it was with the full agreement of the nest.

We will return to Earth. There, we will seek out the Church of All Worlds, though it may be known by another name. The account of Michael's discorporation was written many years ago and the church may be known by another name. The Congregation of the One Faith,

The Temple of the Great Pyramid, the Brotherhood of Baptism—these names were recounted by the historian, Heinlein. Our water brothers may be known by any name, but we will find and join them. I can think of no other higher purpose. When we are ready, we will move the ship to Earth orbit, and seek out our brothers. Until that time, we will continue to practice as Michael taught.

Acknowledgements

Two versions of the novel, *Stranger in a Strange Land*, by Robert A Heinlein, were used in the writing of the story, *The Ship of All Worlds*. The first edition of *Stranger* was published in 1961. Heinlein worked on the novel for the better part of a decade, waiting for society to be ready, or more receptive, to receive the work. It was a long book (about 800 pages) and his publisher asked him to cut 80,000 words, which he did. However, upon his death, his widow, Virgina Heinlein, took advantage of a change in copyright law to publish the longer manuscript in 1991. I read the original version as a teenager, and while re-reading both editions to research my story I was struck by how much it had an impact on my younger self, how he (I) viewed the society around him, and how he (I) developed some of my own values. Whichever edition you read you can't go wrong.

Sometimes short stories inspire a novel, and sometimes there are stories within a larger work. In this collection there are some of the later, that act as ambassadors for the novels in which they reside. *Messages from Afar* is a small portion of the interstellar love story, *The Nyrain Transmission*. *The Shakleton Moment,* two astronauts overlooking a lonely planet far from earth, and *On the Lam* are small scenes adapted from the novel, *MisStep*. Both *Sarge* and *The Runner* are adapted from the novel, *Pemako Burning*. And *The Epistle of Petrit* started life in Book 3 of the *Lucid* Trilogy, *Gods and Dreamers*. There is more about those novels in the end matter of this collection. I hope they encourage you to keep reading.

BOOKS BY CHRISTOPHER MCMASTER

S cience fiction, climate fiction, time travel, alternate realities and more await!

Journey to the Stars

An alien ethnographer collects death moments for his study. One Autumn morning he starts to show Chloe ...

A man's dream of reaching the lights he has seen in the sky, of journey with them, turns to nightmare when he finally gets what he wants ...

With an asteroid hurtling towards the planet, a ship is sent to evacuate a colony. There are some that don't want to leave ...

In the early days of NASA they thought the vast expanse and solitude would be too much for the human mind to handle. For this space trucker, maybe they were right ...

And more! Eighteen science fiction stories from the bottom of the ocean to the depths of space. With a unique look behind the scenes in a conversation with the author.

MISSTEP

A *Stepping Novel*

Stepping: The easiest way to get from point A to point B is to put A and B in the same place. Simply Step from one to the other.

Jens needed to get off the planet in a hurry so he took the first job on an interstellar freighter he found—part of a convoy to a far-flung mining colony, three Steps and almost three thousand lightyears away. Only the desperate went so far—colonists willing to trade a life on Earth for a new start on a rock somewhere across the galaxy, or spacers one step ahead of the law.

But as each Step takes him farther from home, Jens learns that the job isn't exactly what he was told, the cargo not as legitimate, and his situation even more precarious. Jens finds himself being groomed for a role in an interplanetary drug racket, with no way out.

Then the convoy mis-Steps, emerging lightyears off course, and the miscalculation might not be their fault!

seeders

A *Stepping Novel*

After the apocalypse, the flight.

The ocean world is gripped by a pandemic that annihilates everything in its wake. In a desperate act to save their species a remnant of survivors is launched into the depths of space. Frozen in cryo-sleep, they would only wake if their ship detected a habitable planet. But there was no sanctuary, and they continued into the cold and dark.

Centuries later Earth's dream of finding her sister planet has come true, and it looked like it was free for the taking. But buried in the ruins of what was once a mighty civilization, evidence of the original inhabitant's risky mission is found.

Two species are about to collide and the survival of one is at stake!

Pemako Burning

A Stepping Novel

Pemako, an ocean world hundreds of lightyears from earth and the only habitable planet found by humanity. Immigrants soon claim it as their own.

Then something dropped out of the sky. The impact released enough energy to boil the ocean. The ensuing tsunami swept over islands. Death and devastation followed the great wave.

It wasn't a natural even.

Forced to flee their homeworld centuries earlier, the Ruan have returned. And they want their planet back.

American Dreamer

*T*he Lucid Series Book 1

Can one person change a reality?

Chicago. 1944. Waking in a dream Nadia finds herself in a class with two other students. The woman posing as their teacher, (if indeed she is a woman), convinces them that they have no real choice but to assist with her plan. Miss Biel breaks each of them with terrifying nightmares, and 'tasks' to complete while awake that destroys any hope of escape.

But Nadia begins to realise she isn't quite alone, not exactly powerless, and that there are those besides Miss Biel who want a certain outcome. There comes a time when she has to decide who to trust.

American Dreamer weaves present and past in a narrative that transports the reader to an earlier age, and slowly wakes them to an alternative reality, not too distant than our own present.

Tomorrow's History

*T*he Lucid Series Book 2

Can one person save a reality?

London. Present day. Sunlight glints off solar panels, harvesting the energy that keeps the city moving. Roof gardens add a hint of green to the skyline. Airships pass overhead on their way north to the capital, Jorvik. Ships of the Great Fleet load at the busy docks, preparing for the voyage across the Western Ocean to the Far Settlements, holding the Norse world together.

Jakob thinks his world is safe. But it isn't. Something needs finishing for his present to come to pass, and for some unknown reason he has been chosen to do it. Trapped in his dreams, and thrust into an age of Vikings who are much more familiar with the sword and the axe, he uses the only thing he has—his wits.

Tasked with leading a party of Danes in pursuit of royal game, he is swept into an adventure that can only have one outcome if Britain, and the Danelaw, is to survive.

GODS and Dreamers

*T*he Lucid Series Book 3

Time kills all things. Even the gods. That's why they interfere so much.

Three dreamers, manipulated by the gods to play with fate and shape reality. But as each becomes aware of their role, they are recruited into an unseen war, and taught how to fight back.

Together they struggle to protect their timelines and resist those that use mortals as their playthings. Each from a different reality, they must fight to protect what is theirs.

Only first they have to survive. There are others who think them heretics and will try to stop them at all costs.

Pirates Come Down

*F*ishing in the near future takes more than a net!

While some countries fished their stocks to oblivion, New Zealand managed theirs. The nation put a quota on target species, managed and researched it. At the same time, they continued to give the market what it wanted and to pocket the profit, making the nation rich.

But as fisheries elsewhere played out, New Zealand waters started to look more attractive. First, foreign boats encroached, shouting insults, cutting nets, ramming ships. Then they packed guns, which meant Kiwi fishers did too. Vessels were boarded, holds emptied. Fishers killed. Eventually, every ship protected itself with its own PAC, patrol and attack craft, with missiles that skim the surface, and kamikaze drones equipped with explosives.

Only there is a bigger shadow on the horizon, one that defects all radar, is lethally armed, and takes what it wants.

THE NYrian Transmission

After three hundred years of travelling across the expanse, it finally reached Earth.

The first signal was brief, and once deciphered consisted of three words: "Message to follow". The second took longer to decode, and was a detailed tutorial of an alien language. In the third message, the Nyrians introduced themselves.

In response, humanity sent two ships: The Concurrent mission travelled three hundred lightyears to see who was still there. The Response team folded both space *and* time to find out who originally sent it.

Both were unprepared for what they found.

TO Learn More ABOUT CHRISTOPHEr'S BOOKS, VISIT HIM AT:

www.christophermcmaster.com

* 9 7 8 1 7 3 8 5 9 6 5 5 3 *